"You will emerge on the other side of this book laughing, crying, and braver."

LORETTE C. LUZAJIC, FOUNDER AND EDITOR OF
THE EKPHRASTIC REVIEW

"Carolyn Russell's collection of multi-genre flash gives her readers big surprises in small and smartly crafted morsels, deftly conjuring whole worlds and unforgettable characters in fewer than 1200 words."

CONNIE JOHNSON HAMBLEY, AWARD-WINNING AUTHOR OF
THE JESSICA TRILOGY

"Carolyn's insightful voice is both strange and familiar, finding the humanity and humor in lives real, imagined, and in between."

DOUG MATHEWSON & SALLY RENO, EDITORS OF *BLINK-INK*

"Akin to spending time at your favorite art museum. You turn a corner and are greeted by a wall lined with exquisite miniatures, and here, you turn a page and melt into micro-jewels."

JOHN MCCAFFREY, AUTHOR OF *AUTOMATICALLY HIP*

"Russell's collection of compressed literary art is just that: art. Brush strokes trimming out tantalizing microfiction in tighter spaces... gorgeously imagined and thoughtfully rendered."

KEITH HOERNER, FOUNDING EDITOR OF *THE DRIBBLE DRABBLE REVIEW*

"Worlds recognizable enough to feel familiar, yet filled with the underlying dread and longing inherent in our human condition... combines parable, humor, logic and fairy tale to an entertaining and eerily devastating effect."
ANDREA CASWELL, SENIOR FICTION EDITOR OF *CLEAVER MAGAZINE*

"These stories are compelling, provocative, and a wholly immersive experience, even in a medium that celebrates brevity... don't just entertain; they make you think."
BOB KRASNER, 2023 NYPA AWARD WINNER FOR ARTS COVERAGE

"Surprising and teeming with wit."
IAN M. ROGERS, AUTHOR OF *MFA THESIS NOVEL*

"The big bad wolf, a jealous bridesmaid, a distraught mother, and a silver bullet wielding realtor... reimagined fairytales, mini horror stories, and heart-breaking slices of life... clever flash fictions from the first word to the last."
JOAN WILKING, AUTHOR OF THE AWARD-WINNING NOVELLA *MYCOLOGY*

"These deliciously witty flash tales conjure up worlds in a wide range of genres... these sumptuously satisfying stories will haunt you."
MARTHA ENGBER, AUTHOR OF *BLISS ROAD*

"Carolyn weaves a tapestry of captivating tales that push the boundaries of imagination. Brace yourself for a literary adventure that will leave an indelible mark."
SHANE O'HALLORAN, FOUNDER AND EDITOR OF *FICTION KITCHEN BERLIN*

About the Author

Author and educator Carolyn R. Russell lives on and works from Boston's North Shore. Her literary interests are varied, as one might expect given the breadth of genres represented in *Death and Other Survival Strategies.*

CarolynRRussell.com

DEATH

AND OTHER

SURVIVAL

STRATEGIES

Carolyn R. Russell

www.vineleavespress.com

Death and Other Survival Strategies
Copyright © 2023 Carolyn R. Russell

All rights reserved.
Print Edition
ISBN: 978-3-98832-028-5
Published by Vine Leaves Press 2023

Cover design by Jessica Bell
Interior design by Amie McCracken

For Joan Rubin

Ah, world, what lessons you
prepare for us,
even in the leafless winter,
even in the ashy city.
I am thinking now
of grief, and of getting past it.

Mary Oliver

Fairytale Wedding

Ollie was to marry Henry the following afternoon, and we wedding partiers were more than a bit tipsy that night. My three fellow bridesmaids were all from the same Upper East Side castle-dwelling-in-the-winter, Hamptons-in-the-summer crowd Ollie had run with her whole life. I was a grateful outlier, her best friend and roommate at Barnard, which I had attended on scholarship. But by the time we left the restaurant and hit the clubs, I felt like I was on the inside; invincible and unshakable.

It was between Moscow Mules and EDM beats that I found out that there was a posh send-off for Ollie and her new husband the following evening, after the reception. A family tradition. I wasn't sure how I had missed the memo, but as I listened to the discussion of who was wearing which designer, it dawned on me that I hadn't brought anything to wear to this stealth shindig.

I excused myself and swayed to the ladies'. I wet a paper towel with cold water and stood still for a moment or two, pressing it against my wrists so as not to disturb my makeup. A woman I hadn't noticed stepped towards me from a corner nook of the powder room.

"Pick something," the woman said.

I stared at her.

"Make a wish, and I shall grant it."

This city.

The woman looked perfectly normal, impeccably groomed and coiffed. Like maybe a rich matron slumming it with her friends for the evening.

"I want the dress of my dreams," I said. I curtsied as I left, laughing.

The story about meeting my fairy godmother in the restroom was a hit back at the table. In the limo on the way to Ollie's parents' house, I belatedly realized that though I hadn't meant to, I'd gone and confessed my ball-gown deficit. Ollie's crew had been sweet about it, though. And if I needed to double up on something I'd already worn, it wasn't the worst thing in the world.

I woke up the next morning with a very nasty hangover. Not surprising, given that I'm usually a beer and wine kind of minimalist. As I headed to the shower, I was still a little drunk. I took my time under a scalding spray designed to reupholster my dignity. It was a big day, and I wanted to enjoy it.

Ollie's brownstone looked enormous from the street, but even so, from the outside it was hard to imagine it was large enough to contain what the family called The Great Room. Many generations had been wed there, and I could see why. The space was thrilling, with floor-to-ceiling stained glass windows and chandeliers that threw shimmering arrows of light against brocade-covered walls. Ollie looked like a princess, dazzling as she and her Henry murmured their promises and took their vows.

The reception was held in the same hall after nearly invisible staff swiftly rearranged it. The celebration was glorious, with toasts from people whose names I dimly recognized as intellectual celebrities and a small orchestra so guests could dance. And the spread was insane, hundreds of small plates pre-filled with food that looked too pretty to eat. I couldn't help but wonder how the evening's pre-honeymoon soirée could possibly compare to this one.

We bridesmaids eventually retired to our rooms to rest up before the final round. As I entered, I saw something draped over the foot of my bed, something shining and frothy and dark red. When I reached to touch it, I found my arm swallowed up past my wrist by gossamer fabric so delicate it appeared to pulse along with my heartbeats.

The gown was like nothing I'd ever seen up close. The fabric seemed to gather the light to itself and beam it back tenfold. I looked at the label, itself a work of art, with scrolled lettering stitched onto a piece of velvet shot through with gold threads. I didn't recognize the designer's name. It was exotic, with combinations of vowels and consonants I didn't know how to pronounce.

There was no note or card.

I wondered who among our cast of bachelorettes might have been most likely to have loaned me this beautiful thing, who in the group had heard my drunken admission and had acted so kindly upon it. I resolved to find out.

I could barely feel it, the dress was that soft in my winter-weathered hands. I carried it to each of my new friend's rooms in turn. The reaction was the same at each door: appreciative oohs and aahs and, it seemed to me, sincere professed ignorance as to its origins.

Of course. There was only one person it could be.

I found her in the hallway outside my own room, ready for the party and coming to see me, she said. She looked at the dress cradled in my arms and the color rose in her cheeks.

"Oh my lord," said Ollie. "Where on earth did you find this? What an extraordinary shade!"

I held the gown up to her shoulders. Ollie was set aflame, its hue perfectly offsetting her auburn hair and the emeralds at her ears.

We were the same size and had similar taste; during our school years we had freely combined our wardrobes. That I had always benefitted more from this arrangement had bothered me. Now was a chance for me to repay her, and I wouldn't take no for an answer. We would trade clothes for the evening.

The dress fit Ollie as though it had been sewn while pressed against her skin. Its bodice clung to her ribcage, somehow suggesting the curve of each delicate bone beneath the gleaming scarlet silk. The same fabric cupped her breasts before curving into a high, Victorian-style lace neckline. Beneath her slim hips, the gown increased in volume: billowing panels of paper-thin velvet that just skimmed the floor. The dress was objectively demure, I knew, yet on her, it seemed more revealing than sheer nakedness.

When she and Henry appeared at the threshold of the ball, I swear there was a collective gasp. They appeared to float toward the dance floor; once there, they melted into each other's arms.

Ollie stopped breathing several minutes before midnight. She died in full view of more than a hundred people, after silently falling to her knees. The autopsy revealed no previously undetected heart defect, no underlying illness. There was some scant evidence of constriction at her throat, but nothing definitive.

We go back to that nightclub as often as we can. We recreate the circumstances, drinking Moscow Mules and dancing to whatever happens to be on tap. And I go to the powder room, hoping to find the woman who furnished me with the killer dress. No luck so far. But my Henry and I are determined to find her.

He wants revenge. I want my next two wishes.

TRIQUETRA

She asked me to write postcards to her, because she loved them, because they reminded her of better times when she would gather her long cotton skirts together and shape them into stiff feathers of lonesome clouds like Stevie Nicks and say she wanted to rock my gypsy soul and spin with her arms over her head, her hands like the shimmer of stars that beckon to sailors in the frail pink light of evening's end. I took her to appointments and we passed the bottomless hours deep inside our San Francisco tales even though they were now decades old and one of us had died already and maybe that was part of why, and when time ran out we talked about what message did I have for him, and we wondered if the bedroom eyes that got him sick were still as long-lashed and if he was beautiful still, as he was when we were three on the floor at the I-Beam on Haight Street dancing to "Every Breath You Take" and dreaming it'd always be like that, gold, gold, golden and I never wrote the damn postcards, at least not more than a couple of them before forgetting to remember.

BARGAINS

My wife had recommended a website her friends use to find bargains. They send me an address in a neighborhood that they say is close by. I've never heard of it. But I'm more than game. Our microwave is shot, and I'm desperate. Turns out, we use it nonstop during the day without much noticing. Both of us are working from home now, and the full-time togetherness is beginning to really piss me off; having to warm up my coffee in a pan on our stovetop is the shitty cherry on top. And I miss my Hot Pockets. Yeah, I know. First-world issue.

"Some people have real problems," my Gina says to me at least three times a week. And fuck yeah, it's annoying to hear. But she's usually right about most things, and she's right about me. I am that guy. So what.

We decide to walk because I've been bad about exercise the last couple of months. Even more so than usual. Gina wants to take a wagon with us, the one we use to haul debris off our property after a Nor'easter, but I nix that. I'm still capable of walking a few blocks with a box, and I tell her so. She does this thing she does, squinting her eyes to keep them from rolling. I pretend I don't see it and grab her by the hand. Maybe a little too roughly, but what the hell. She works out all the time; she can take it.

About fifteen minutes later, I'm sweating like a pig when this frail old woman calls to us from the front porch of a triple-decker.

"You here for the oven?" she yells.

"The microwave?" says Gina.

"Yeppers," says the lady.

"It's here?" I ask.

She ignores me and looks at Gina. "You sure you want it?" she says. She cocks her grizzled head to one side and stares at my wife.

Gina goes completely still then. I've only seen her like this once before. It was at our engagement party, five years ago.

You gotta understand: Gina is the definition of perpetual motion. She's got more energy than you can even imagine. She says it's the special smoothies and ointments and candles she gets from her friends. They reek, by the way. The crap she brings home from her buddies, who all smell like they just took a bath in some toxic swamp. Gina does, too, but better somehow. Maybe I'm just used to it.

So, at the party, when I saw her centered in a half-circle of girlfriends toasting our marriage, and she suddenly went all frozen, I noticed, even from across the room. One of the women said something, and they all burst into laughter, and Gina laughed with them. Her eyes found mine, and she raised her glass to me. A second later, they all did.

"Gina?" I say now. Maybe a little irritably.

She shakes herself out of whatever state she's in and turns toward me. "You sure we need this, Honey?" she says.

"What the fuck is your problem?" I hear myself yell. I say some more stuff, too. It's true; I have a short temper.

Gina tells the lady that yes, we want it, and when the box is loaded into my arms, it's heavier than I thought it would be, and the cardboard is chafing against my skin after just a few minutes. I wish we'd brought the wagon, but I don't want to give Gina the satisfaction, so I don't say anything. Instead, I keep my eyes down and pretend I don't need to be balls to the ground somewhere soon, or I'll puke up breakfast.

Score another one for Gina. Right again.

It's a lot to live with.

When we finally get back home, Gina asks me what I want to eat for lunch, a frozen chicken breast or a salmon thing. You might think Gina would be a kickass cook with all the herbal tinkering and potions she and her crew make, but you'd be wrong; we spend a small fortune on premade meals. I say salmon, and she hands me a package from the freezer and tells me to just press the fish button on the new/old microwave.

Turns out, I like the water. I enjoy breathing through it, swimming in it, and floating while watching Gina dance around the living room on the other side of the glass.

I'm glad I didn't ask for chicken.

COMMUNION

A seagull tiptoes towards me with short, tentative steps, her tracks a sandy geometry of renounced solitude. I throw her a few potato chips, but the creature doesn't move; her red-rimmed eyes stare into my own. I understand ... my puny reparations are laughable. The gull's face is suddenly illuminated; the plump dishwater clouds have parted and scattered. The beach is transformed, an ambered postcard, every rock and stem and wave redefined by an alchemy of salt and sunlight. An ordinary miracle, sufficient unto this day.

CHERRY BONES

Judging from the angle of sunlight playing with my cat, Taro, I've had a bit more sleep than I am usually able to manage. I wake up in sections, stretching on the expensive mattress my kids insisted I needed; they were right—rising is a lot less painful than it used to be before the something-o-pedic. My hips take the longest time to cooperate, and because I need them to sit up, I thank them first. They're not perfect but they're the original set, and that's more than a lot of people my age can say. I am grateful for every part of this body for what it continues to give me, and for what it hasn't. At least not yet. So, I start each day voicing my thanks out loud, a ritual Taro has come to believe is Taro-centric. She thinks most things are.

• • •

I sit at the edge of my bed and grab some woolen socks from the basket that hangs off the wooden headboard. This is the most irritating part of my day. My feet have never been anywhere close to pretty, and the past twenty years have not been kind to them. More disturbing than the way they look is their increasingly sinister unreliability. They have a tendency to seize up or go numb when I least expect it, that is, when I forget to remember their intermittent treachery. They are my anatomical problem children, and, I admit, it's a struggle to love them. Especially when just putting on a pair of socks can be so tedious; my toes balk at the necessary contractions, and the rough, calloused skin of my heels catches on the soft alpaca Nordic designs my youngest daughter favors. I sportscast the process for Taro, who listens closely while quietly attending to her own velvet paws.

• • •

When I am able to stand, Taro performs figure eights around my ankles, her tail flicking at the damp flesh behind my knees. She ushers me towards the hallway, then leaps ahead. As I shuffle into the kitchen, Taro jumps onto the countertop where she stalks the electric can opener. Unlike a lot of cats, she never feigns indifference. Taro is an unabashed lover of life, a Zen master of moment-to-moment mindfulness and grace. I have been a most willing disciple.

• • •

I've been saving some fresh cherries for this morning's breakfast, a treat I enjoy both for their sharp, sweet flavor and for the memories they conjure. When my girls were little, they'd called the stems "the cherry bones." They'd wash them in apple cider vinegar and collect them in a special jar. When they had a decent amount, and when my eldest declared that it was time, they'd bury them in the backyard under our copper beech tree. Always the same spot. Nothing has ever come up. On fine days, though, Taro and I pick our way through the bright shade of the tall green grass and check. Because why not?

• • •

Taro watches me abandon the dishes in the sink without washing them. I don't mind leaving them dirty, and I know she doesn't either; she likes to poke at them when she thinks I'm not paying attention, hoping I've left something good for her to chew on. I feel unusually tired, kind of a bit wavy, actually, and I sit back down at my place at the end of the long farmer's table. My middle daughter will be along soon. I think I'll ask her to check my blood pressure. She's a veterinarian, not a doctor; we always enjoy trading jokes about the medical care she gives me. I'm wondering what we'll make for lunch when a jagged blade tears at my side and I call out for Adrienne, now ten years gone, and m ...

• • •

Taro is licking my face, the part that's not mashed up against the chilly Mexican kitchen tile carefully chosen for its beauty and affordability when our house was in the planning stages. I'm glad of its cool comfort. I'm flat and feel like I've been pasted against one of those outlawed playground spinning saucers, but I've nothing to hold onto. I'm just whirling, afraid that if I lift my head from the floor, it'll stay still. I may choose to linger a bit, right here, and rest my cherry bones.

SOMETHING BLUE

"It's my first wedding," gushes my client. "I want my gown to be really special." Her mother nods in agreement.

Shockingly, I am no longer shocked.

I retrieve the marked tape looped around my neck and grab a sharpened pencil. But it's just for show. I've already taken her measure.

Agave Cotton

Our first night together was all jalapeño pepper-infused tequila and impulse. Passion came the following morning when I fell for his sheets. They were crisp but soft and smelled like something pure, like rain, like a freshly baked biscuit. So did he. He still does, I'm sure. I'm not sure.

In a New York Market

Nina willed herself to say nothing. She piloted her emptied grocery cart to the collection area and launched it into the rusted corral. Squeezing her eyes shut, she tried to erase what she'd seen.

A woman in her early twenties had been entering the market as Nina left, and their paths had crossed for an awkward moment before Nina straightened her cart's wheels. The woman was dressed in monochromatic oversized clothing and sneakers; a Red Sox baseball hat crowned red-rimmed, exhausted eyes. An infant carrier straddled the metal edges of her cart's top shelf. Fabric covered the overhang and protected the baby from the cold.

Nina wished she could have seen the infant's face. Shopping was a chore, but the sight of other people's children was a joy, and one that soothed her newly empty-nested soul. Her second thought plagued her. The smooth plastic surfaces of the carrier seemed precariously balanced on a rickety cart which, even when it was new, had no business holding a baby.

She and her Samantha had been lucky, but she'd live with the cries of her child tumbling backwards over a slick metal panel for the whole of her life. That, and the triangular scar above Sam's left eye, a delicate geometry that had saved her vision. The surgeon had been sympathetic, but Nina never forgave herself. Though she had meticulously researched the baby gear she bought, she had blindly trusted a grocery store contraption. Familiarity bred assurance.

Nina went back to her car. If her kids had been with her, they would have pleaded that she resist the impulse to interfere. Paul would have told her that, statistically, the child would be fine. But statistics meant nothing if you drew the short stick, even if you had no idea you were gambling.

She found the woman in the meat aisle, heading towards the hamburger.

"Hi," Nina began. "I hope you don't think I'm crazy. I just wanted to warn you about these grocery cart deals. They're really not approved for this kind of thing …" Nina gestured toward the baby. "There are a lot of problems with kids being injured when carriers slip off the front section, and I hope you don't mind, but I just wanted to mention it. Most folks just assume that they're safe because why else would stores encourage it, right? But …"

Large double doors behind them opened, and a white-uniformed man emerged from the back of the supermarket with packages of wrapped beef that he placed in the freezer in front of the two women. The blast of cold air that came with him lifted the infant carrier's flimsy protective flap.

Nina stared into the carrier's interior. No baby. No baby, but several jars filled with the store's brand of strained carrots, diapers, and some cans of evaporated milk.

Stepping between the butcher and the woman's cart, Nina reached out and pulled the thin fabric covering back over the front of the carrier and pressed its bottom corners against their worn Velcro fasteners. She looked up to find the young woman's eyes on hers. They rested there, a benediction. And for Nina, a release.

She smiled back before retracing her steps down the aisle and out the door.

Full Moon

Jill asks me to meet her at the town golf course. It's the middle of January and freezing cold, but she's more sister to me than cousin, and the raw urgency in her voice scares me. When I get there, I go to the low benches that front the whitened green. They're icy and bare, treacherous. Shielding my eyes against the setting sun, I scan the expanse of snowy acres. I see her then, my Jill, on a small incline in the middle of the course. She extends an arm when I reach her, the one not holding the baby.

"Stay back," says Jill. "I don't know how bad it is yet. They might be able to get inside your head, too, if you get too close."

I know, right then, that things are never going to be the same again, that my life is now forever split: what came before and what came after.

"What can I do?" I ask.

"Take Vivi. I don't think they know about her yet."

Jill darts forward and thrusts the baby into my arms before backing up several feet. Vivi is pale and shivering, maybe too cold to cry.

"My car's really close," I say. "Let me take you home, Jill."

"NO!" she screams. "They can hear everything there!"

She runs towards a copse of evergreens, away from me and the baby. I look at Vivi's little face, all scrunched and wet, and sprint to my car. The formal adoption comes through when she turns three.

Half a decade later, my wife Katie and I throw Jill an engagement party for her and Stewart, an older, easy-going guy. It's nice. A small group of family and friends, hors d'oeuvres and cake, and honest joy for the couple. Especially for Jill. She's been through a lot.

There's a full moon, and I go outside to smoke a cigarette. I hear footsteps behind me; Stewart has joined me on the deck. He puts his hand on my shoulder, and I turn toward him.

"Don't worry," he says. "Her doctors are really pleased with Jill's progress. We'll be fine."

"I know you will," I tell him. "As Jill must have mentioned, we're always listening. You're great together."

I stay outside for a while before I rejoin the festivities. Jill and Stewart are waltzing in the living room. Vivi watches from Katie's lap, her head nestled in the tender hollow between her mother's chin and collarbone. I catch Stewart's eye; he avoids mine. I cross the room to my family, and then it's the three of us, my whole world.

"Kinda wonderful, isn't it?" says Katie.

"Sure is," I say. "A lid for every pot, I guess."

"Speaking of which, would you mind starting the coffee?"

"Already done," I say.

"See that, honey?" Katie says to Vivi. "I've always said your dad's a mind reader."

I hear Vivi laugh as I go to fetch her a second glass of lemonade; she's feeling too shy right now to ask.

TWO CUPS OF COFFEE

I arrive early and sit at a table with a view of the sidewalk just so I can do this: watch as Mark lopes toward the diner, his bow-shaped mouth in full pout. He shakes his head, crosses the street, and stares into a storefront's reflective glare. A minute or two later, he comes back. With the full weight of his shoulder, he swings the door open; its belled frame shudders and clangs.

He makes a beeline for me and slams his way into a chair.

"What the fuck? What's so damn important you had to call the *house*?" he half-whispers furiously.

"I've emailed, I've texted, I've called. Nothing from you," I say.

"Right," he says. "Because we've been nothing since your profound revelation or epiphany or some such shit. So, what? Your karma decided to give you a free pass when it comes to my married ass? Good for you. Except I'm no longer interested."

Mark gets up, like we're done, like he's calling the shots.

"Sit down. I need to tell you something important to both of us. Please don't make this any harder."

He does this thing guys like him do. He grabs his chair and turns it backward at the table and straddles it, facing me, like his throbbing manhood must be fenced in, contained, lest it wreak havoc upon the place.

"Go ahead, Annie," he says. "This can't be worse than our last little meet-up. 'Cause that was fun. Big, big fucking fun. Ask my wife."

"I'm sorry," I say. "I'm sorry for everything. I'm glad she decided to stay."

Mark stares at me, those emerald greenies more eloquent than he's ever been. He rubs the blond stubble on his face and takes a deep breath.

"What is it?"

"I've been contacted. Rudely. By our former... mentors," I tell him.

"That's impossible," says Mark. "Are you sure?"

"I'm as sure as I can be, given the circumstances."

"Mary, mother of ..." His right hand curls into a fist.

"Yes."

A woman with a metallic briefcase enters the restaurant and sinks into one of the cracked leather booths near us.

"How could you let this happen?" says Mark.

"Say something unexpected. Just this one time."

"Fuck you," says Mark.

I make a show of looking around, my gaze lingering on the newly occupied booth close by.

"I'm not sure we should be talking about it here. Why don't we ..."

Mark interrupts me. "I am never. Going anywhere. Ever again with you. Not even around the corner. So let's get on with it. I have to leave soon."

"There hasn't been a day I haven't regretted..." I begin.

"Shut the hell up! You have no idea what ... just tell me why I'm here now or I'm gone."

"Yesterday I was mugged," I tell him. "At least that's what I thought was happening. After I got home and cleaned up, I realized that the guy hadn't taken anything, he had given me something. In my handbag. You can guess what."

I watch as Mark digests this news. In a near-hilarious tell, he swipes at a trace of phantom cocaine beneath his nose.

"Christ," breathes Mark, and he closes his eyes. "I guess you expect me to handle this. It's not like you've ever been into getting your own hands dirty."

This bit is certainly true. It's how I've stayed alive in a lethal line of work.

Mark stands abruptly, and his chair smacks against the table. He stalks toward the restrooms and barrels through the swinging double doors.

While he's gone, I make a quick phone call to The Accountant. When I look up, Mark is at the counter. He brings two cups of coffee to the table and places one of them in front of me.

"Still sugar, double cream?"

"Touching, you remembering that," I say. "So, we do have some options."

"Not so much," Mark snarls.

I take a small sip of coffee. It's very bitter, like my cold, dark heart.

"If we work together ..." I begin.

"You really want to go there? Look, I can't stay. Gotta be somewhere. And I need to think."

"I'll call you," I say.

Mark's baby face flushes. "Don't. I'll get in touch with you when I'm ready." He raises his cup and waves it dramatically. "Salut!" he says. He takes a long pull of his coffee. I bring my cup to my lips and pretend to swallow. "Like I said," Mark says, "I'll be in touch." He pins those Irish eyes on mine.

I flutter my eyelids and angle my head slightly before I let it begin to droop slowly toward the tabletop. Mark catches my cheek in the palm of his hand and eases it onto the surface, and Jesus, the touch of his skin on mine, even now. I hear him walk away, then listen to the belled door do its thing.

The gunshot is loud enough that my fellow diner patrons jump to their feet. A woman screams, and there's a lot of shouting. A few people have rushed to the windows.

"Fuck me, that guy was just in here!" says one of them, a guy with a salt and pepper goatee.

"Well, now he's all over the sidewalk," says his pal.

Amidst the commotion I slowly raise my head. The first thing I do is rub my lips and tongue with a napkin;

my signature crimson gloss glows bright against the white paper. I spit a couple of times for good measure.

I check my phone and find that The Accountant has left me a message: *debt paid in full.* His version of mission accomplished. The palm tree emoji at the end of his text tells me he'll be out of pocket for a while.

As I leave, I dump the poisoned liquid out of my coffee cup and put both cups in my carryall. A girl can't be too careful.

BORDER TOWN

Chatham Falls was the kind of leafy town that announced itself with an elegantly rustic wooden sign as motorists crossed the bridge over the tidal river that bordered its realm. A minute or two later, the driver would notice another sign, this one gesturing toward the municipal equestrian field's parking area. And its historically registered clubhouse. And that, mused Ava, was everything one needed to know about how much a good realtor could make here, if one were willing to deal with the locals, who were insufferable.

Her thoughts were interrupted by two stragglers emerging from a red Tesla. Ava suppressed a sigh and snuck a surreptitious look at her phone. Only five more minutes and the open house would officially end. It had been a long day and she was ready to go home; her fiancé would have dinner waiting. Nevertheless, she straightened the lapels of her corporate-issued blazer and crossed the darkening front lawn to greet the newcomers. *Good bones*, Ava thought the man in hipster sunglasses responded. His companion, a young woman in a full-length rain slicker, nodded. They went through the front door, signed the call sheet in the foyer, and walked past her into the living room.

Ava supposed they meant that they appreciated the house's structural design. She herself didn't much care for the neo-Gothic aesthetic of the place, but it was her job to sell the property and she didn't need to love it to be effective. She checked the sheet for their names: Julian and Angel. Ava called out to them but heard nothing.

The interior had become gloomy despite her best efforts to light the place up with a cheerful glow; her own room-flattering candelabra bulbs and candles were no match for the home's murky mahogany paneling and heavy furniture. She made a note to bring in some floor lamps for the next showing.

Ava heard a thump from the upstairs. Lord, she hoped these two weren't like the weirdos she'd once found screwing in the master bathroom of a vacation cabin. At least they had ended up purchasing the place.

She checked the time again on her way up the stairs to find them. Twenty minutes past five. She called out their names and waited, but a thick silence had settled between the walls of the old house.

Irritated now, she searched for the couple.

Ava found them in the guest bedroom. They had wrestled a large antique sea chest from its place at the foot of the bed into the center of the room and had removed the blankets it had held. They stood facing her from behind the empty trunk. *Yes*, Angel said, angling her head towards Julian, *good bones*. She was holding a carving knife, and it occurred to Ava that the woman had dressed perfectly for this occasion. *You may begin*, the man said, adjusting his spectacles.

Ava groaned. This kind of thing was becoming all too common, and if left unchecked, would certainly depress property values. She withdrew a sharpened wooden stake from her sleeve, but after getting a closer look at the couple, dropped it in favor of the silver-bulleted, small-caliber Smith and Wesson she kept in her pocket.

Afterwards, Ava called her office. "Two more. 190 Fort Pleasant Avenue," she said. "Hazmat suit-level stuff." Then she called home to say she was going to be late, and please could there be stiff martinis when she got there? Ava turned off the lights, blew out the candles, and adjusted the central air to as cold as it could get. It was October and chilly outside, but she knew the cleanup crew would thank her for it. She locked the door behind her and exhaled. She'd give the bridge troll double what they asked for tonight, she decided. For luck.

Dawn's Early Light

Shane had convinced her: that he was kind, that their fates were entwined, that he wasn't like those creeps her mom breakfasted with on weekends. Liv couldn't save her mother, but she could save herself. That she was now running for two was a wild card she'd figure out later.

DISTANT, SOCIALLY

I press the garage's remote button and say aloud, "I'm closing the garage door." I rap my knuckles three times against the steering wheel. As my Subaru crests the top of the steep driveway, I look back over my left shoulder. The broad door is still closed.

I drive with care. If I hit the slightest bump, it'll set me back timewise, as I'd need to pull over, get out of the car, and visually inspect the area to make sure I hadn't hit anything. Sometimes I need to check twice.

The Dollar Store is only a couple of miles away, but I get stuck in the wake of a school bus and curse my luck. I hate forcing the drivers behind me to wait while I count to twenty after the last child is safely inside, but only then can I let my foot hit the gas pedal again. Thankfully, the bus stops only once before I pull off the road.

The store seems to be busy, its parking lot crowded, and I fight the impulse to go home. Just fifteen minutes. Fifteen minutes and I'll be done for a week or two.

I find a spot and wedge in between a motorcycle and a white minivan. I try hard not to make the connection between it and the van I drove years ago. Too late. I bite down on the inside of my cheek so that I don't evaporate into memory. The salty taste of my own blood is usually enough to do the trick, and it works this time, too.

Head down, I keep my eyes on the pavement and my feet moving, hoping the momentum will keep me going. I reach for the large glass door festooned with posters and ads and realize, belatedly, that these had blocked my view: as I step forward, I nearly collide with an older couple on their way out. I apologize and we dance around each other, bound in opposite directions.

I grab a bunch of store-supplied alcohol wipes to use on the handle of my cart: three swipes, back and forth. Finished, I try to move quickly, but it's hard to get through the narrow, messy aisles without nearly grazing somebody's arms or shoulders. With my free hand, I hug my overcoat closer to my body.

I have a list. Paper towels, napkins, Lysol spray, garbage bags, soap, hand sanitizer, and some other small items. I run out of these things so quickly, it's too expensive to buy them online. Searching the shelves, I will myself to block out the middle-aged woman and her elderly mother as they make what passes for conversation in their world.

"Don't even touch that, Mom. It's nasty," says the younger woman.

"It's pretty. It reminds me of the sky," says her mother, showing her daughter a pale blue and yellow polyester scarf.

"It's pure crap," says her daughter. "Put it back now!"

"Then why are we here?" wails the older woman.

I don't wait to hear if there's a response. I head to the back where the discounted cleaning supplies are. The plastic containers all have colorful off-brand labels that suggest the designs of their more famous counterparts. It's my favorite section of the store.

A boy of about six or seven appears at my elbow and lightly touches my fingers where they grip the elbow of my coat.

"Are you cold?" he asks.

I can't help it—I jump out of his reach. Why do I even bother to shop during school hours if parents can't be counted on to follow the rules? The child's eyes are huge, liquid brown, his smile missing a front tooth or two. My Jamie would be about his age now.

I abandon my cart and run into the parking lot. I lean up against a cement-potted pole and wait for my heart to slow down and my vision to clear.

The trip back home isn't too bad, the traffic sparse and orderly and smooth. I pull into my driveway and inch down its snowy slope, my foot on the brake. Once inside the garage, I close its door electronically and sit, caught in the spiky embrace of the cold darkness. After a while, I lock the car and head inside. I pause on the stairs to rap my knuckles three times against the wood-work and say, "I've closed the garage door." I look back over my left shoulder to make sure.

Inside, I take off everything I'm wearing and put it all into one of the large plastic bags collected for that purpose. I carry the bundle into the laundry room and put it in a hamper. Securing the door behind me, I head to the bathroom.

I avoid my reflection in the mirror. My eyes land on a pack of disposable razors instead, and I almost choke out a laugh. I step into the shower and absorb its obliterating scald. Not nearly hot enough, but the best I can do.

A Dish Best Served Cold

Damn. This season's stepdad was home. Predictably, John was both drunk and stoned. Some things you could count on.

"Ella!" John yelled. The sound of her name in his mouth was nauseating. "Where's my Arby's? You eat it? Girl, I swear, that answer better be no!"

She and her mother were strict vegetarians. This fact seemed to frequently escape him, unencumbered as he was by any real working memory. She did hope he'd find the sandwich, though. She'd spent hours curing its meat and mayo under the brutal Florida sun. If he ever called her spoiled again, she'd just laugh.

August and All That

White-nosed and Ray-Banned, the summertime soldiers stalk across the beach, resplendent in their neon orange swim trunks and gleaming neck whistles. They eye each other, keeping track, keeping score. One of them is kind, but not so kind that he can be bullied. From him, I'll learn to stay adrift.

THE TWO SISTERS,
FRAMED IN THE LOUVRE

It vexed me no end that we were often mistaken for twins. That the years of experience and maturity that separated us went unrecognized by so many casual observers gave me heartache, for though I loved my sister dearly, we had taken very different paths in life, and I was unseemly in the pride I took in my own.

What did the eye apprehend in our presence? Two women of age. My sister levels her gaze serenely at our audience, secure in her position, but less sure of my own; she grasps my arm firmly, an attempt to hold me back from a die already cast. She refuses to acknowledge the pale rose at my hand, pinned there this very morning by Sophia, my love. My sister's willful blindness is tempered by fear, I know. But it is still an effort and a heartache to withstand her resistance.

From the throngs who crowd us daily I understand that things have changed. I might have been afforded the comforts of transparency had we been of this wild age. Instead, I dream, and accept the tender mercies that are my due.

Packing It In

All we had in common were a neighborhood and kids who were the same age and took a class together. But it was me Rachel called the afternoon before she left her husband. I wasn't surprised the marriage was over; Zander had never bothered to hide his serial cheating and it was a much-discussed, open secret in town. Just surprised she called me.

I knew she wanted to make it a thing, like you see on TV. Laughing, crying, margaritas, and junk food. But we really weren't that close, and though I liked her and admired her, it was weird she wanted me with her as she packed up essentials and put together boxes of memorabilia. I asked if I could help; she said I was helping by being there for her, which made me sad. We barely knew each other.

The last time I'd seen Zander was at the local ballet studio, where our kids, barely out of diapers, dressed up in fairytale clothes and skipped in circles. They loved it. Their daughter had stopped to help mine with a shoe-lace issue. I was trying to tell him this nice thing about his kid, but as soon as I mentioned her name, he interrupted me. *What did she do?* he asked in an aggressive baritone, like he was talking to the police. I couldn't imagine what living with the guy must be like. I told my Danny about it when I got home; he just laughed and told me I didn't realize how lucky I was.

I watched Rachel unload her bookshelf in the bedroom, slowly, volume by volume. Mostly poetry, mostly women, a lot of mid-century stuff in the Confessional mode. She held each book in her two hands for a moment before fitting it into one of the small, sturdy boxes that littered the rug. She broke her rhythm to wave a slim hardcover in my direction. Sylvia Plath. It was a signed copy, a gift from him, she said, angling her head towards the windows, as though Zander might be out there, bobbing his head against the glass like a balloon.

Rachel was upset, sure, but also befuddled by the latest turn of events. Rumor had it that Zander had spent all their money behind her back on some sketchy tax scheme of some sort. Since she was the family's main breadwinner and had spent many years before their late marriage working overtime at a mangy law firm outside the Beltway, this amounted to nothing less than legal theft.

"Love," said Rachel. "The great pretender."

I didn't know what to say to this, so I just sat there with what I hoped was a receptive expression on my face.

"The truth," she said, "comes at you sideways, in little packages, delivered in between shallow breaths. Grief, too."

I nodded and mumbled something about her having a way with words I envied. I told her I'd refresh our glasses, glad to escape.

I took my time on the staircase, studying the family photos that line its walls. They looked like ours, everybody happy, everybody beaming their appreciation of the good life into the camera lens. I straightened a couple of picture frames and picked up a stray ponytail holder on the landing before heading to the kitchen. It was kind of a mess, dried-up food stuck to cereal bowls along the counters and plated sandwich crusts and murky half-filled tumblers on the table. I scraped the dishes and put everything into the sink to soak before going to the refrigerator for our drinks.

Behind the pitcher Rachel had prepared was half a pizza wrapped in cling plastic, and I grabbed that, too. I carried our drinks and the food carefully back up the stairs, past all those smiling eyes. The last thing this house needed was another mess.

Rachel had moved on from the bookshelf and was sorting papers at her desk. She looked up when I came in and motioned for me to put everything on a dusty bedside table. I unwrapped the pizza; I hadn't realized how hungry I'd become.

It was a pineapple, bacon, and broccoli pie, a combination that turned my stomach. My husband's favorite.

Sometimes he added mustard just for fun to see me fake gag. I must have made some sort of noise because Rachel came over and stood beside me.

"Yeah," she said. "I know. Disgusting. Danny called it brain food. The two of them were at it again a couple of nights ago, trying to figure out this IRS issue. Is the rest of the cheese one gone?"

I said I'd check and went back down the stairs and out through the front door and kept on going. I took some shallow breaths.

FOLIE À DEUX

My wife comes in and says, *I've got to ...*, as she slaps her palms against the kitchen tabletop and dangles her head between her shoulders and groans. I wait politely for her to finish, even though I know she won't; I'm used to these episodes. She'll say, *I've decided I'm ...*, and *I can't believe that ...*, and *Jesus Christ, it's ...*, that sort of thing, and then stop, and then I'll prompt her to say more, and she'll look at me like I'm nuts, or she'll get angry. At first it was merely annoying, but eventually it became maddening; I came to believe that she did it on purpose to keep me off-center. When the truth hit me, it was hard to take—it isn't about me because I don't figure into her considerations, like you don't consult the bug on the windshield before you go through the carwash. *You've got to what?* I ask.

SEVENTEENTH AND CLAY

When my housemate came home, I was doubled over on
top of the monstrous 1940s-era heater that dominated
the second floor of the flat we rented with two others.
He was my least favorite of the bunch, a wraith-like
art student at San Francisco State whose rabid love life
was broadcast to us all through some strange alchemy
of architecture and passion; in the mornings we'd have
to face breakfasts with sketchy strangers nursing their
hangovers with warm beers left out the night before.
He noted my posture and asked if I was okay before
moving on down the hall toward the bathroom.

I didn't feel okay. My body had become unfamiliar
in ways that scared me. My nipples burned so much
I couldn't wear a bra, and the smell of the popcorn
constantly on offer in our kitchen kept sending me out
onto our rooftop. There wasn't much up there, a couple
of ragged lawn chairs and a milk crate. The view was
spectacular, though; the house perched on the top of a
hill halfway between The Haight and Twin Peaks, and
the city unfurled endlessly below its ragged Victorian

splendor. It was to the roof that I lurched that afternoon to contemplate my options.

My live-in boyfriend, Perry, was my second lover; I had been twenty when I had sex for the first time. Not that my relatively sheltered adolescence absolved me of any responsibility. In fact, the enormity of physical intimacy was what had kept me virginal for so long. That and abject terror. I'd never been the most confident person in the world.

And so, the first thing I thought about was jumping. The second thing was this anti-drug movie called *Go Ask Alice*, last seen in my early teens. Why? I think maybe because all the stuff I'd been warned about doing my whole life was what I'd been doing within weeks of arriving in San Francisco. It was all one big, bad thing: the sex, the weed, the nights out dancing in unsavory neighborhoods, the play I was in that ran from midnight to two a.m. four times a week. Pregnancy seemed like the inevitable fate I'd been running towards. I fell asleep thinking of baby names.

When I woke up Perry was in the chair next to me, beer in hand. He didn't need to ask if I wanted one; in those days, I never wasted calories on alcohol. I told him everything. He held me in his arms, said something that made me laugh, then cry a little.

The next morning, he went to work. I took the day off. I remember that I took the bus to a drugstore in a different neighborhood, which makes no sense to me now; our friends were based all over the city, and I knew no one who lived close by. It must have seemed like the right thing to do at the time, something gleaned from a film or TV. I bought a test and took it into the restaurant next door. I ordered coffee and drank it as quickly as I could. Then I headed to the restroom. The stick changed color.

Out on the street again, the sun seemed ridiculously bright. I found a phone booth and slammed my way into it. I called Paula, one of three close friends from college; we'd followed each other out here, each of us doing what we could to pave the way for the next East Coast arrival. Paula picked up immediately. She always seemed to be there when I needed her, and she was there for me then, her old-style Yankee calm pragmatism undercutting any drama I might have been prone to.

That evening, Perry and I had dinner with what Perry described as our "best couple"; he had this theory that once you're part of a relationship you date other couples and eventually find a match. Nell and Ranney were ours. I had met Nell through work, and the four of us clicked almost immediately. We spent holidays together, went on movie marathons and to galleries, and stayed up late talking art and music. They were four or five years older than us, around twenty-six or seven, and I adored them both. We told them about the pregnancy and the decision we had made hours earlier to end it. I was only a few weeks along, there was no way we could care for a child, we weren't ready to marry, etc.

I went home that night and sobbed.

A week later I interviewed at the city's department of social services. Nell and Ranney had told Perry and me that on my meager salary I could probably qualify for financial assistance with the medical side of things. And I did, but not until after filling out a lot of paperwork and succumbing to an intrusive array of questions, surrounded by throngs of people whose problems seemed exponentially worse than my own: the desks were all bunched tightly together, and the sonic waves of human misery were inescapable. Shame washed over me, and I thought of my parents, wondered if I'd ever tell them.

The procedure itself wasn't too terrible. The doctor and nurses at Planned Parenthood were kind, and it was quick, so quick.

When Perry and I got back to the house, Nell and Ranney were waiting on the flaking front porch we shared with the downstairs tenants. As Perry fiddled with the door lock, a stab of pain and nausea hit me, and I stumbled on the threshold. Perry caught my elbow. "Stop it; you're fine," he said. "Actresses," said Ranney, and Nell punched him playfully on the arm.

I went to lie down. From the bedroom I could hear the three of them, laughing and telling stories. It wasn't the worst betrayal that would explode us, but it was the first, and the one I remember the most often, all these years later.

ON THE 495 NORTH

We've not moved for ages.

"What's the square root of New Jersey?" asks my daughter from the back seat.

"Hmmm," I say solemnly, as though this is the kind of question with which I grapple every day. What might the answer be? Springsteen?

I could sit in traffic all day.

LOVELY IN THE DYING LIGHT

The three of us were, at that point, used to sidestepping our mother and relying on our stepfather, Sam, to keep us in the loop. The last few weeks, his emails had become shorter and more alarming. Mom wasn't taking her psych meds; she was drinking again; she was leaving the house when he wasn't paying attention. She had threatened him with a steak knife. After that last one, I got panicky. Especially since Sam wouldn't write me back, not even to ask for more money for a new specialist or better help around the house.

I'd also been trying to reach my sister for days. No luck. Keira was the yin to my yang, though, always adventuring about. She was probably off camping somewhere, out of range. I was the mellow twin, the one who'd rather curl up with a good book and a glass of wine than almost anything else. Or, if you believed our brother, Tom, I was the sensible twin, the one he didn't need to worry about.

I called Tom, finally, though I knew he was on a business trip to the West Coast and too far away to do much more than worry along with me. He didn't pick up, so I left him a message. A long one, telling him about my plan to drive the 500 miles to check up on Mom.

I traveled through the night and arrived just after noon. My seaside hometown looked idyllic in the pale gold light that shimmered off the marina and spilled onto the shoulders of the lunch-seeking tourists. I opened the windows and traced the town's curvy brick streets; the salt air was glorious, and I let myself relax, a rehearsal for the nap I planned to take as soon as I could.

Before our father got sick, he had lovingly renovated a stately Federal in a shady older neighborhood. From my car, the place looked a bit rundown, its white columns smudged and chipped. Two of its black shutters had peeled away from the brick façade and anguished towards the hydrangea bushes below. I parked in the back, adjacent to what Keira and I used to call our "twin-splace"; one would never know from the sidewalk that this secret expanse of yard was geographically possible. I wanted to linger there, but instead padded around to the front of the house. Here was something new: a brass knocker in the shape of a ram's head had been nailed onto the wooden front door, which desperately needed a coat of paint. I wondered, not for the first time, what the hell Sam was doing with the funds my sister and brother and I sent him every month.

I had to wait at least three or four minutes before I sensed movement behind a first-floor window. Still, the door stayed closed. I'd brought the keys I kept for emergencies. As I extended my hand towards the lock, the door swung open. Sam stood in front of me, shaking and wild-eyed.

"I killed you already," he said.

Behind him on the floor was Keira's backpack, the fancy waterproof one I'd given her for our birthdays. It was unzipped. Nearby, a lipstick and a pair of rolled woolen socks were splayed across the foyer's scarred pine boards. I slipped and fell to my knees in something sticky, my fingernails scrabbling for purchase. I heard a sickening thud. My last conscious thought was for Tom: *Don't come here.*

We all watched the trial from the rafters of the Suffolk County courthouse in Boston. Our father, an attorney while he was alive, explained that the change of venue was more than warranted given the amount of local fuss over our murders. Tom didn't think it had much mattered in the end. The city jury convicted Sam on all counts except those pertaining to Mom; her body was never found, which created some technical issues with her case. Occasionally, we've tried to figure out its location, but it's no use. Mom can't remember anything.

In the evenings, we gather around the fireplace out of habit. Eventually, Keira and I drift out to the backyard, not because we were both buried there before the police came and found us, but because somehow it still feels magical, its sweet earthen perfume as intoxicating to us now as when we were kids. The house has finally been sold at a discount to an intrepid buyer with a young family. It's our hope that one day soon, we'll share our garden with children. Maybe it'll become their favorite place, too. Like our town, it's especially lovely in the dying light of day.

THE BLOUSE

I struggle out of a thickly layered dream; something shifts in my chest and grows heavy. My mother is shaking my arm. I can see by the faint light the moon is throwing through the bedroom window that she's got her scary smile on, the one that says she's being reasonable, it's us that are crazy, driving her to say and do things she wishes she didn't have to.

She wants her blouse back.

What blouse, I ask, trying to focus. You know, she says. The blue one with green flowers on it.

This is a blow, as I have eaten myself out of most of my own clothing and need this top that my mother, in desperation, has bestowed upon me. Her thinking is that it's ridiculous to waste good money on clothes that won't fit me in three weeks and maybe having nothing to wear will motivate me to be more sensible.

She says again that she wants her blouse back. Now.

I look at my alarm clock. It's 2:45 am. I get out of bed, trying not to wake my sister on the other side of the room, and find the blouse in my closet, paired with a faded denim skirt. My outfit for school tomorrow. I hand it to her, and she does this thing I dread most, a stiff-necked nod meant to convey that okay, we're square, all's right with the world. I get back into bed.

In the morning, I know, she won't say a word to me, and I'll be invisible to her for three or four days. Maybe longer.

I Know What
You're Going to Say

I know what you're going to say. I should have known better. I should have been smarter. But I didn't, and I wasn't.

It was a book launch on the Upper East Side that brought me out that night, away from the coziness of the boiler room I rented in Brooklyn and called my apartment. It was hot in the winter and reasonably cool in the summer, and on occasion I had fit as many as seven people into it. It wasn't the smallest place I'd been in since I'd moved here.

The launch was for my friend, Liv. We worked together at the lowest level of a rabid but sadly popular magazine; our beat was a thin online version that nobody read. Liv and I were close in that way that similarly minded people sometimes are, cheering each other on sincerely, but keeping a close eye on each other's progress. It helped that she was a writer and I was an artist, working with lino and gel prints; we each had our own bailiwick. But I can't say I wasn't a bit rankled that evening. Liv's book was a kids' thing, 500 words and 32 pages. It was simply written and illustrated by a grad-school friend of hers. It had been picked up by HarperCollins.

I know what you're thinking. You're not wrong. I maybe had a bit too much to drink at the party, enough that when the event ended and shifted to Liv's agent's apartment in the Village, I got into the limo.

I had met this agent several times before; when I grew up, I wanted a life like hers. Her name was Natalie Chase, and she lived with her husband and a couple of kids in a seven-room compartment of a brownstone that had been in his family for generations. It was all real oriental carpets and original artwork and space, space, space.

Have you ever lucid dreamed? That thing where you're in a dream but you know it, and you can alter its elements in a hazy semiconscious way? That's how I felt when we got to Natalie's. Instead of joining the group in the living room, I found myself wandering around, touching things. The polished oak paneling was butter beneath my fingertips, the silken lampshades dimpling as they met my knuckles.

When I felt a hand at my elbow, I knew it would be Liv. I was having a terrific time, I assured her. Liv's eyes were wet and half-closed by then, like they couldn't bear the light. We walked arm in arm to where the group was preparing a final toast. As the fluted glasses were raised, I put my arm around Liv's waist. She put her head against my shoulder and smiled up at me.

I know this sounds terrible, but of the two of us I was the most sober. So, after we made the rounds, hugging and thanking everyone, I made the Uber call while Liv got our jackets. They said it was going to take a while because it was so late. Ten minutes or so later, we were on the sidewalk, swaying slightly in our spring dresses, waiting for a white sedan and a guy named Steve. When the car pulled over, I helped Liv into the back seat. I had left my purse behind; I handed Liv my jacket and told her that I'd be back in a minute.

Can you imagine it? Running up the stone steps, going back to Natalie's, explaining, finding my bag, and racing back down again to find the street empty and quiet?

She made a call that night. The police won't say to whom, only that it lasted a few seconds. Uber says that their records indicate a no-show at Natalie's address on the evening in question.

People were wonderful to me during the first few months of Liv's disappearance. Natalie and her family were amazing; they took me in while I went through the worst of it. I'm actually still there; the kids and I became very attached to each other and I've sort of become their nanny/de facto auntie. Natalie has put me in touch with some of her contacts, and my prints are beginning to receive some notice.

I know, right? Everything happens for a reason.

LUNCH TICKET

Something shiny fell out of Michael's pocket on the last day he drove me to school. He was ahead of me, halfway across the front lawn when it happened, a gleaming that streaked from the pocket of his gray hoodie into the new snow, where it sank without a sound; I picked it up as he stomped his feet a few times against the driveway hardtop and unlocked the car door, and I hid it in my backpack before he turned his head and gestured for me to hurry—my brother had the new grin on his face, the one he aimed in my direction without seeing me. I waited until lunch to investigate; in the girl's room I found a stall with a lock that worked, and standing with my back to the door, I brought the thing into the light. It was a silvery metal rectangle with rounded corners, like a container that had been mostly flattened, with a cap that I unscrewed and sniffed at; the stuff inside smelled brown and made me gag, but daring myself to taste it, I filled my mouth with the liquid before spitting most of it out into the toilet and going back to class. My parents were called into school soon after my math teacher leaned in close over my shoulder. In the principal's office I offered no explanation, no defense; I watched my dad's Adam's apple go up and down and my mom's fingers twist together in her lap, but still I said nothing, aiming my face in their direction and swallowing hard against them, the rough fire still alive on my lips, a ticket out of a place I couldn't name.

TILT-A-WHIRL

It was 1969, a tough time to be the only chubby kid in an athletic family. I had no idea then how many of the emaciated fashion models and actresses I adored were desperately ill with anorexia. Much later, we'd learn it boasts the highest mortality rate of all psychiatric diseases.

Not that it would have mattered to my eleven-year-old self. Back then, I would have done almost anything to be as thin as my idols. But I'd have gladly settled to look like one of my svelte sisters. Or my mom, whose figure in all the fancy white tennis clothes she wore made me proud. My sisters and she shared such outfits, body-skimming tight-waisted micro dresses that came with ruffled underwear that was meant to be seen, and tiny skirts that looked like they belonged to paper dolls.

I sweated out that summer in a pair of my father's rolled-up running pants and an oversized tee shirt. It wasn't the most comfortable way to run around the hot clay courts my family favored, but it was better than the alternative: showing my limbs in public.

The day we all went to the Eastern States Exposition, I had picked out roomy jeans and a poufy hippie top to wear, which I covered with a long button-down cotton shirt. I was armored up and ready to party as only a sixth grader can: carnival rides, cotton candy, and goofball games that earned winners plush prizes.

It was a great day for a fair. The air was replete with the mingled aromas of popcorn, fried dough, and the kind of ketchup-sauced pizza we all put up with in those days. I ate a lot of all three, as did my three siblings and parents; it would take a while for me to make a true connection between what I ate and the way my body looked.

My little brother was the one who discovered the two attractions in a side alley. One was run by a muscular man in a sleeveless undershirt, which I'd only ever seen anyone wear on television. He was in charge of a huge mallet that he loaned for a price to willing strangers interested in proving their physical strength. If the participants bashed the large button on the ground with enough force, a red disc would zoom up to the top of a flashy vertical tube and ring a bell. It was fun to watch.

After a while we moved next door, where an entirely different kind of challenge was featured. A whiskered man in a mangy suit stood next to a gigantic glitzy scale and bellowed for players. For a price, he would guess your weight. In front of a crowd. If he was within three pounds, he won. If he lost, he'd pay you back double what you'd spent.

I'm not sure whose idea it was to volunteer me. But I remember someone saying that he'd never guess what I weighed, and that we could win and spend the money on more rides. It didn't occur to me to say no. That's not who I was.

Up close, the barker smelled like sweat and something I'd identify years later as whiskey. He didn't smile at me or make eye contact. He went right to work. He pushed my shirt sleeve up to my shoulder and then stared at my bare flesh before closing his two hands around the widest part of my arm. He told me to relax, and he took my forearm and flopped it around, weighing it in his head like our butcher did to hamburger before putting it on the deli scale.

The man told my parents his guess. And ordered me to get on his oversized scale. The machine's blinking lights bothered me, and I closed my eyes. When I opened them again it was because my dad was calling my name.

We had won.

As we trudged back to the rides to spend the prize money, I lingered behind. My brother stopped walking and waited for me to catch up. When I did, he slipped one small hand into mine. With the other, he dug around in his pocket until he fished out a ragged square of pink-wrapped bubble gum. He handed it to me with a devilish grin; our parents had expressly forbidden us to chew gum while on anything moving fast, lest we choke on it by accident. I gave him back half, and minutes later we were on the Tilt-A-Whirl, risking our lives together for a taste of sugar and the weightlessness of centrifugal force.

GROUNDED

It's not that difficult to get things into the ground, my grandma had told me every spring. It's getting them to come back up, to reach for the sun, that was the hard part. I hoped she was right, and that what I'd just buried would never see daylight.

Dinner alone was strange, but something I felt I could get used to. I was draining a second glass of wine when I heard the thunderclaps, followed by the rush of a murderous downpour.

Time will tell, my grandma would have said. I sincerely pray it doesn't say a word.

RELEASED

The bullet misses her face; it deflects off the bullhorn she holds to her lips. Despite the hole in her lungs, she continues to chant as many hands lift her up and over the crowd. Then she is free, released now, at last, to be the eye, not the storm.

ALL HALLOWS' EVE

Her little monster! Cara smiles as her son wrestles with his decision. What to wear tonight? She's happy that she's made sure he has options. The head is a foregone conclusion, but Cara has worked for weeks constructing several plush outfits that would both terrify his peers and keep nine-year-old Logan warm on this chilly October evening. Now he gazes at them, his ferocious energy directed toward making the right choice. She has fanned out the meticulously made costumes at his feet, the old lime carpeting competing with the shaggy surfaces of Cara's handiwork. The colors make her eyes hurt a little.

Logan looks at his mother. "Which one do you like best?"

"Well now," Cara answers carefully, "the orange one took the longest time to make, so I guess I'd like to see it get some action, but I think they're all pretty good."

"The best so far!"

Cara grins at her son's enthusiasm, but it's also a bit worrisome. He's been especially keyed up about trick-or-treating this year, and she doesn't want his energy to flag even before night falls. He's not like other kids his age; she's got to manage these things. As so often happens, he catches her thoughts.

"Don't worry, Mom! It's only one night a year."

Thank goodness for that. One is quite enough.

Logan beams, his little face glowing.

"I'll be right back," she tells her son and goes quietly down the cellar stairs. The smell of the place is strange this time of year: dust and mildewed stonework mixed with the solutions she uses to vanquish the worst of Logan's clothing stains. And something else, below the surface of those odors. She locates the old freezer in the gloom; it's flush against the moldering back wall, beneath a nearly opaque window. She pulls on the ancient cord above her head, and the overhead light blinks on. Next year, Logan will be tall enough to reach it himself. The thought brings tears to her eyes. His childhood is flying by.

She needs to check that the ancient appliance is still plugged in and humming; Logan likes his treats cold. She hoists the freezer lid open and peers inside. It's frosty, but just about empty. Well, that's what Halloween is for, right?

Entering the living room again, Cara sees that her son has struggled halfway into the orange outfit.

"Almost dark!" she calls out.

A low growl of frustration emanates from Logan. Too soon. Not yet. Not even out the door. She crosses to him and sees his problem. The back zipper is caught, and she fixes it, allowing Logan's shoulders to slide inside the furry suit. She settles the fabric around the back of his neck and his head pops out. He is dressed.

"All set," she reports. "You good?"

"Yeah!" he yells. "I'm ready to go! On my own tonight, right?"

"Right," says his mother.

Cara feels a bit dizzy, suddenly overwhelmed by memories of many other such evenings. She'd pace herself tonight, maybe try to catch a quick nap before Logan comes home. There's always so much to do at the end of the holiday.

Cara follows her son to the foyer. She smooths his hair, nearly giggling at the backs of his ears; she's never gotten used to their pointy angle. Logan turns toward her before reaching for the front doorknob, and she evaluates the look she's created. She smiles. The costume's orange color exaggerates the neon amber of his eyes, while the knives she has sharpened and fitted to the ends of each gloved finger echo the shape of her child's razor-edged teeth.

With a wave, he is out into the night. Logan yowls, a screaming affirmation of his mounting bloodlust. The sound is joyfully repeated, its replication a new game for the stream of children trick-or-treating on the sidewalk. He slips seamlessly into their midst, and Cara sighs. Her baby, growing up so fast!

UNDONE

Tires spin, my truck floating and weightless. The sky blooms against my windshield, and I'm sailing as pixelated dreams sing to me, a staccato rat-a-tat-tat of what I've left undone, unsaid, untried. A false flag looms, the jaws of frenzied whitecaps. I cover my eyes, but my hands stay still.

NYC 1987

Bright red plastic tape crawls all over his hospital room door, and the words on it don't matter; its warning is clear. A nurse with comb-over eyebrows sees us paralyzed in front of it. "You can wait inside," she says. "He's having some tests done." She manages to both smile and look terrified. "We keep the door closed because, well, who knows?" *It isn't airborne* is on the tip of my tongue, but my husband squeezes my hand, and we just go in.

Road Show

Something was wrong. I brought my car to a full stop behind the heavily branded corporate van ahead of me. We were near the center of our small coastal city, and this kind of stoppage in the middle of a well-trafficked main road was strange. Then another same-company van that had been heading toward us halted; the left-side windows on both vehicles rolled down and, elbows out, the two drivers began to converse.

It was a beautiful spring weekday, and I was unencumbered by gainful employment; a perfect day to wander and gawk at all the emerald newness. I had nowhere to be and didn't particularly mind the delay. Glancing at the rearview mirror, I noticed a car had pulled up behind me. The driver looked like he minded. Maybe very much. As the minutes ticked by, I watched Angry Dude in the mirror. His face was becoming an unhealthy shade of pink as he spoke animatedly to his passenger. He raised his hand in an unfriendly gesture.

We were now stacked four or five vehicles, all of us waiting in place, engines running. Up ahead, the two van drivers continued to chat. I wondered how long it would take for someone to start yelling or exit their car. Angry Dude seemed like a prime contender. I picked up my cell phone. It just seemed like the thing to do.

Just then, I caught some movement out of the corner of my eye. To the right of the van ahead of me something was moving, *very* slowly, across the road. The object became more visible as it cleared the van's right front tire. And then, it came into full view. A tremendously huge tortoise was making its ponderous way across the thoroughfare toward a bordering swampy pond. It was a magnificent creature. Black and gold mud looked bedazzled onto its shell; shades of greenish muck on its torso and tail glinted in the sunlight. Head down, the animal crept diligently toward its goal, oblivious to all else.

I looked into the rearview mirror. The guy behind me was smiling and pointing out the tortoise to his buddy, who leaned out of his window to look. The van in the opposite lane moved forward, its driver giving us all the classic thumbs-up, a huge grin on her face. The van in front of me waited for the tortoise to get within a foot of the grass line that surrounded the water, and then it, too, was in motion. We all gave the animal a very wide berth as we passed, our cars now a celebratory parade.

I've often since thought about that day, about how limited our individual perspectives are, and how, as a result, how fragmented must our notions of the truth be at any given time. Context and angle govern our reaction to events, the equivalent of squinting through a spyglass when what we need is Google Earth. I've been back several times to that pond, hoping to catch a glimpse of that tortoise again, with no luck. Apparently, he was a one-epiphany-per-customer kind of fellow.

My Zaide's Golem

I'm seven years old when my great-grandfather tells me about the family golem, about how in the old country they would conjure this thing out of mud that would protect our ancestral village from pogroms. "Tell him the rest," my dad says. And then I learn the bloody cost of coaxing such a creature into being from a circle in the dirt. I can't understand most of what Zaide is talking about, but I know that I am being asked a question. I say, "No." I want nothing to do with this savior. My dad carries me in his arms and cries all the way home.

RECEPTION

She had found them at the bar, two men in their mid-thirties knocking back whiskey at her best friend's memorial. She looked from one to the other. "Are you the good brother or the bad brother?" she asked.

The panic on their faces was gratifying.

They'd both been *very* bad brothers.

THE CALLING

Sarah was sore in body and spirit as she rode Zed into town. Sarah turned the horse onto a shortcut through an alley. The windows of a first-floor photography shop mirrored their dusty progress, and she looked away. The blood on her shirtwaist and cloak was far more extensive than she had supposed.

She'd lost both of them, mother and child, to a form of fever she'd seen before, but could neither prevent nor cure; there was nothing in her vast store of midwifery experience or anecdotal memory that could account for this plague. The gasps of the mother's final breaths as she reached for her child, born still, echoed in Sarah's ears. She laid her head against Zed's shaggy mane and let herself weep. The horse slowed.

"What would you have me do?" he said.

"Let us move on," said Sarah. "Food and water are running low. We may yet receive another Calling."

"We?" asked Zed.

"You. You, you insufferable beast." Sarah half-smiled through her tears. Trust Zed to bring her back, always, from the brink. His gift and her skill had bound the pair in their dangerous vocation since she was a girl. He knew her like no human ever had.

The sound of shouting male voices roused Sarah from her reverie. She looked up. Three o'clock in the afternoon or thereabouts. She steeled herself for whatever would come next.

Tombstone. It was a dusty boomtown not unlike so many others she and Zed ministered to. The place epitomized a certain ethos. The coercion of metal out of its rocky womb was Tombstone's prime occupation and obsession, and most of the town's violent proceedings could be traced to this pursuit.

"Hold steady," Sarah told Zed.

She reached for the Derringer in her left boot seconds before the group of men appeared at the mouth of the alley.

"Do you recognize any of them?" asked Sarah.

"Nay," said Zed. "But I know their souls."

Zed moved sideways in a quick motion, drawing close to the wooden panels that fronted a small saloon. The medical bag that Sarah kept strapped to her saddle struck this flimsy wall with a dull thud.

"It will be fine, Zed," said Sarah, anticipating his question. "The medicines are well-wrapped."

Shots rang out. Sarah made herself as small as possible atop Zed. Her gun, were it to be espied, would make her a target in this circumstance, and she buried it in a deep pocket. She laid her face against Zed's neck and waited.

It was over quickly. Sarah, used to timing birth pains and heartbeats, figured this gunfight took about 30 seconds and cost as many bullets. Zed nickered, and Sarah looked up. A thin man with a handlebar mustache lurched toward her, bloodied and limping.

"Mercy," the man moaned, reaching out, gun still in hand.

Sarah dismounted and caught the man as he stumbled. She propped him up against the front wall of the saloon before moving toward Zed. The horse backed up and stomped his left foreleg.

"Nay," he said.

"I need my bag, Zed. He is bleeding."

The horse shook his head almost sorrowfully, but firmly. "The Calling has nothing to do with the likes of this gentleman."

The man with the mustache gaped at Zed. His eyes rolled back in his head then, and it seemed his consciousness was lost. Sarah crossed back to him and checked his pulse; still alive. She removed the bandanna from her neck and twisted the fabric to increase its bulk. Sarah pressed it hard against the man's seeping hip wound.

A new man appeared and yelled to his companions.

"Doc Holiday's over here! Wounded bad!"

Two other men ran to where the injured gunman lay. Together, they hoisted him up and arranged his dead weight near vertically between them.

"Wyatt?" said one of them.

"Take Doc 'round back and bring him upstairs; he's got a room here. Get the surgeon," said the tall man who, apart from his peers, appeared completely unharmed. The others nodded and went about their task. When they were a little ways away, the tall man turned.

"Much obliged," he said, executing a small bow before following his friends.

Sarah watched him for a moment before turning to Zed. He met her eyes with an unblinking stare.

"I cannot be a part of these doings of men. Pray, do not ask me again," said the horse.

Sarah mounted Zed and scratched him between the ears.

"Let us find provisions," she murmured.

"We need to make haste," said Zed. "A Calling this way comes."

SUBURBAN

The leafy main street of my town was as familiar to me as my own bedroom, every driving inch of it fortified with layer upon layer of muscle memory that guided my hand as surely as I was able to brush my teeth each morning despite Carson screaming, swearing at the top of his lungs about whatever was his target of the moment. Sometimes me, sometimes electronics gone wayward, sometimes an early work email. I'd long ago resolved to ignore it, keep my head down, and wait for it to pass. It always did. His mood would unspool like a string of Christmas tree lights, first a bit, then all at once.

Today the road was amorphous and strange. Houses I'd driven past a thousand times looked a new shade of their former selves, as though some artful force had draped a caul over the weathered clapboards and spilled an amber tea over the lawns and shrubberies and three-car garages. Even the school kids spilling from open doors before being shepherded through the crosswalk seemed contrived of watercolors. The sight ignited an old sorrow. Carson had changed his mind about having children soon after we were married.

I was marveling at the sepia-toned town square when the Suburban ahead of me slowed down enough to make me lean on my brakes. I came to a full stop when I saw the car's bumper stickers: two black and white exhortations to co-exist and vote. I had the same ones on my car, and in the same locations.

The vehicle also was the same vintage as mine, same make and model, same color: dark green. I'd wanted a lighter color for safety, but Carson had said it'd be too hard to keep it looking clean. So green it was. Not worth fighting over.

I looked at the driver. The back of her head looked very much like my own, a tangled blonde bob of agitated curls I'd been too impatient to tame before leaving home. The woman ran both her hands through her hair now, then tied it back with a band of some sort. She gazed into her rear-view mirror, and our eyes met. Hers were framed by professorial round glasses. Involuntarily, I touched my own. Mine were the same shape, but darkly tinted, a protection I needed against bright light. Carson thought them an affectation.

The woman looked to her right, and it was only then I noticed she wasn't alone. She put her hand on a man's shoulder for a moment. He must be tall; she needed to reach up several inches to make contact. Then she got out from behind the wheel and walked toward me.

The sun seemed to slide then, and drift audibly behind the woman with a sigh. Its radiance burnished the edges of her form and obscured her features, but I'd recognize that face anywhere. I left my car to meet her. She handed me her keys and something else before she passed me.

I walked on, pulling my hair back into a ponytail with the elastic the woman had given me and slid into the seat she had vacated. To my right was Ian, my college boyfriend, who smiled when he saw me and asked if everything was okay. The car behind us moved forward and accelerated. Then it was past us. I watched until it crested the hill that marked the beginning of the corn-fields that bordered our sleepy town and disappeared.

I told Ian everything was perfect.

WAITING ON THE WORLD TO CHANGE

At the dollar store, her cellphone pings and she reads the online responses to her query about what time the lab opens at the city hospital's satellite office. One guy says, *Why don't you just call them?* She wants to say, *I'm alone. I'm scared. I'm at the dollar store.*

Rhetoric 101

I lean toward Sophie and re-cross my summer-bare legs, hoping she'll notice the new heels I thrifted online. Vintage Betsey Johnson.

Dr. B. drones on, something about using specific details in our writing. Sophie reveres this guy; our whole class does.

I don't get it.

"The tall skinny pervo with gimlet eyes," I loud-whisper at her.

Sophie throws me a wide-eyed angry look.

"Don't you just hate me?" I say.

I love her. One day I'll tell her so.

A Visitation

I hear you, I think, making tomorrow's coffee by the curdled light of the moon. At the sound of glass breaking, I run. Of course, the kitchen is empty when I get there. Still, I brush my hand across the glossy tilework of the countertop. My ring finger comes away bloody.

"Happy anniversary to you, too," I whisper.

Constrained by Love

"If You're Ever Stuck in a Zip-Tie, Here's How to Escape" tops my newsfeed headlines. I'm sure the algorithms-that-be have determined that this sentence will all but guarantee I click through to their ads for medications my doctors don't want me to know about and certified letters from Santa. For years these formulae have ruthlessly mapped my fears for my twenty-something daughters, who live in big cities and regularly walk the razor's edge between a sincere belief in the potential of the human spirit and the dictates of survival. I do my best to resist, but an hour later I consume and forward the article. My daughters will call each other and make gentle jokes at my expense. But they will, I know, read it eventually because they are my children; I'm sorry, you're welcome.

GRIT

The girl was wet-nosed and unkempt, blinking against the cruel light of my cellphone's high glare. She turned her head back into the scarred nylon of her sleeping bag and lay still, as though I might disappear if she could no longer see me. I sat down on the grimy cement stairs a few feet away from her spot in the alley and waited. She seemed to fall asleep after a while, but I checked that she was still breathing every ten minutes or so while keeping an eye on my backpack.

A couple of hours later, she sat up. I went to her and set up my old camping lantern; I studied her by its light as she drew her legs up under her chin and locked her fingers around her knees. Dark smudges under her eyes accentuated glittery cheekbones. Hard to tell if it was makeup or grit.

She watched as I drew some items from my bag. A box of Kleenex, a tube of Neosporin, water. When she reached for them, I tried to breathe slowly. Her inner arms looked almost purple, their long, thin length punctuated by darker spots that clustered near her elbow.

I handed her sandwiches next, along with some multivitamins. I thought I saw a wisp of a smile when she took those, but it was hard to tell, and in any case, the expression was fleeting. I told myself that she had appreciated the irony; it made me feel better to believe she was still in there somewhere.

The girl threw what I'd given her into a plastic shopping bag, either for future use or sale. I had no way of knowing. When she stood, I resigned myself to the end of our time together. As she moved away, she said, "Thanks, Mom."

When I could no longer see her in the gloom, I pulled out my marked-up city map. I found the alleyway on it and drew an X on it in red Sharpie.

She never slept in the same place twice.

But World Enough and Time

My last night on the job at the Not a Thru Way Campgrounds, I was doing what I did every evening: roaming the premises at dusk to check on each site and make sure all was well. Often, I was asked to join folks as they played guitar or swapped stories around their fires. Though I grumbled about these rounds to coworkers, they were vastly entertaining to someone like me.

As I approached my final stop, something crunched underneath my boots. My flashlight's thick beam found I'd trampled on a pile of empty glass cylinders. One of my hearts started beating furiously, but I told myself to calm down. I'd found all kinds of things out in those woods. I made a mental note to clean up the shards in the morning.

The family I found gathered around a timid campfire reassured me. They couldn't possibly have been more typical: mom, dad, teen girl, younger sister, kid brother. And a pale medium-sized dog that shivered nervously as far from the flames as his leash would allow.

We chatted for a few minutes and the mom invited me to sit down and share some toasted marshmallows.

The dad and kids were enthusiastic about this idea, and the boy scampered off to get a fresh stick for me to use. When he returned, his dad told him it was a beauty.

"Thanks," said the kid. "On my planet, this isn't allowed, but I'm okay with it here."

His sisters exchanged exasperated looks and laughed, but his parents played along, nodding supportively. It was clearly not the first time they'd heard this kind of thing from him. I stayed for a couple of treats and headed back to the overgrown shack we called an office.

Not too long later, the boy walked in.

"So ..." He said.

"Yeah." I told him. "How'd you find me?"

The kid snorted, something he must have learned here. "Wasn't easy."

"The dog? Anyone I know in there?"

"He's a new recruit. Not handling the fire thing so well, but a good tracker," said the kid. "Just like you were."

"Won't this family miss you and the pooch?" I asked.

"They won't even know we're gone; we came into their lives a week ago. When we go, they won't know that, either."

"Wow," I said. "The neurotech has come a long way."

"Much improved since you ... left us. No more pesky trace memories."

I said nothing.

"Anything you want to do before we take you home?"

"I'm assuming the High Court hasn't changed its mind? It was such a small, confined blaze, and it hurt no one ..."

The boy shook his head. "Sorry, man."

"I'd like one more night under this moon," I lied.

The boy looked confused. I had learned to tell untruths from humans. I knew the boy was having trouble with my request; he just couldn't figure out why.

"Go get Poochie and do the erasure thing and come back," I said. "One last night, for old times' sake. And maybe you could clean up your neuro-med capsule mess in the woods before someone gets hurt on those sharp edges."

The kid looked stricken; I knew he would. As soon as he left, I retrieved the flask of kerosene I kept in the back pocket of my jeans. First, I called 911. I waited until I could hear the sirens before slopping the stuff all over the floor and furniture. When the alarms got really close, I stepped out the back door and threw a match back inside. The inferno I left behind would stymie the boy and his dog for a while; neither one of them was going to come close to anything like this. We're not built that way, not since the Years of Smoke and Ash. Well, most of us aren't. I seem to have been born without a protective, morbid fear of fire.

My current job is a thousand miles away, and sadly, it's indoors. But I love the daily alchemical rush of turning steel into useful or beautiful forms, and the sparks that fly off my metal tools offer a wild wonder I've never known. My fellow welders think the hours I keep are crazy; I spend almost all my time at work, immersed in the heat and flames. And I wait for the next team to find me. When they do, I'll probably leave this place. There are many worlds to play in.

MAKING WAVES

My daughter is singing. Her contralto is muffled as it drifts down from her upstairs bedroom. As always, I find its guileless vocal fry utterly charming; she sounds world-weary at age seven. I go to the foot of the staircase to listen in and maybe eavesdrop on her and her younger sister, who's five.

If I were a boy, I would sail the seven seas, sail the seven seas, if I were a boy ...

Suddenly my blood runs cold, and my thoughts leap madly in all directions. Foremost amongst them: It's impossible to know how many ways you can fail until you have children. It's the one thing, above all else, that you want to do perfectly. And I've obviously failed miserably in my efforts to raise girls who feel empowered to pursue their dreams.

My husband and I had waited eleven years before we felt we were ready to start a family. We moved around a lot for work in those days, and it just felt practical to delay child-rearing until we settled down. Plus, I hadn't yet formulated my Plan, a coherent philosophical approach to parenting I hoped might ensure that our kids would someday avoid all of my own mistakes.

I time travel back to a day in my early teens. My mother comes home from the market and tells me a story. She'd been at the produce counter trying to find a ripe cantaloupe when a young man appeared at her elbow. When my mother completed her task—sniffing and thumping and performing the other arcane rituals she deployed on a regular basis to choose food she deemed fit for our family—the stranger spoke up: "Would you mind telling me which melon came in second?"

I'm afraid that tale had an outsized effect on me. We had a book of inspirational sayings in our house that I thumbed through whenever I was desperate for something to read. The one that always caught me up short said it's better to teach a person to use a fishing pole than to give them a fish to eat. But I just wanted the fish, not the tedious instructions on how to learn a process I found disgusting. So, I totally got Melon Guy. My mother's story confirmed a dangerous theory: I could let some kinds of things slide and still count on the universe to provide me with ripe fruit.

Unsurprisingly, this perspective proved increasingly problematic and difficult to shake as I grew older. I vowed that if I were ever brave enough to have kids, I'd make sure that they knew how to fish. Especially if they were girls.

Now, hearing my second-grade daughter yearn for an autonomy she seemed to feel was already out of her reach, I am momentarily stunned. Then I leap up the stairs, two at a time, and burst into her room.

"Honey," I begin. "You can sail the seven seas if you want to! You can study and practice and work hard to accomplish anything you'd like! Girls can do everything boys can do!"

I continue in this vein for quite some time, so caught up in my own alarm that it takes me a while to notice that I'm not letting either girl get a word in edgewise. I finally end my impromptu lecture. My five-year-old's eyes are huge, like she's seeing Mickey Mouse's head come off so the actor inside can eat pizza. My older daughter puts her hand on my shoulder.

"OK, Mom," she says. "But I was singing 'If I were a *boat*, I would sail the seven seas.'"

Oh.

"Who's hungry?" I ask, distraction being the last refuge of a chagrined parent. I follow in their wake as they bolt down the stairs, racing toward a future I can barely begin to imagine.

The Way of Things

"How long have you known *her*? Just this summer, right? And how long have you known *us*?" Deenie's bathing suit had ridden up her bottom, and she punctuated her words with angry little tugs.

"Yeah," Evelyn chimed in, her chin trembling.

I was only eleven years old, but even I knew that's not the way love works.

ORCHIDS

I really wanted to like this one. And why wouldn't I? I'd adored my son's other girlfriends, nearly all of them.

Lord knows, he's dated a fair handful.

This one was different. I could tell as soon as she knocked at our front door; her rat-a-tat-tat was loud and impatient. Miles sprang up from the sofa like he was on fire. As he ushered the girl inside, I watched her eyes sweep over the living room, saw her note that the house lacked a proper introductory foyer, the living room instead creeping up to the very threshold upon which she now perched, carrying flowers. Well, excuse me. I'm sorry we don't live in one of those mansions like you see on TV with two-story entryways that lead to shiny appliances and gigantic stocked refrigerators.

She was pretty in an exotic way, I guess, what with her hair in tight dark curls that dripped halfway down her back and her dramatic cheekbones. When she held out the flowers, her hands looked tiny, like those of a child, but they were beautifully manicured, her nails the same color as the trembling blossoms. Must have cost a fortune.

"These are for you," she said with a toothy smile. "It's so lovely to meet you, Mrs. Slayton."

Miles stood beside her, beaming like she'd just mastered cold fusion. "They're orchids, Mom. Very delicate to take care of. But I told her you could handle it."

Then they just stood there grinning at each other, like they had a private joke no one else could possibly appreciate. I reached for the square wooden pot of flowers; it had some sort of foreign writing on it, probably an inane command for the world to be blissful, or maybe flexible. I hear yoga is big these days. I held my tongue.

"Damn, sorry! I haven't introduced you! Mom, this is Amanda. I think I told you, she and I met interviewing for the same job. Turns out, we were both at Northeastern at the same time, but we were in separate programs..."

Blah, blah, blah. I waited until he was finished waxing all poetic about the astonishing events that led up to their miraculous first encounter.

"It's nice to meet you, Amanda," I said. "Please call me Vicky."

I cradled the orchids in one arm against my belly, and I stuck out my other hand. She was a lefty, her hand dry and soft until something bit into the folds of flesh on my palm. I yelled and snatched my hand away and looked at the red indentation on its underside, hoping for blood.

Miles was suddenly beside me. But his arm was still around Amanda.

"I'm so sorry," said the girl. "We were going to tell you this afternoon! I turned the ring around to surprise you later..."

"It's my fault," said Miles. "It was my idea. We didn't want to ambush you with the news until we'd all gotten to spend some time with each other."

I knew it. This one was trouble.

"It's nothing," I assured them. "Come in and sit, please. Let's get acquainted. Or maybe you'd like to show Amanda your room first? We just had it painted. Miles picked out all the colors, his favorites."

The girl turned to Miles. I couldn't see her expression. Miles took her hand and led her up the stairs to the bedroom he still lived in, three years after his fancy college graduation.

They're still up there; I can hear them talking. That's okay. I doubt we'll be sitting down to dinner anytime soon. Truth be told, I hadn't defrosted anything anyhow. What I had done was neatly fold his underwear and socks and place them on his pillowcase. Because that's what good mothers do.

ROUGH PALMS

The woman who stood in the doorway of her Malibu Dreamhouse was all but unrecognizable to me. It was a rather liberating thing under the circumstances. Maybe we could begin again for real this time, me behind my own experienced face, her behind an immobile mask wiped clean of history. Barb had chased success until it finally caught her, and if she chafed under its demands, including the endless ways that she'd been compelled to ruthlessly traumatize her own body, she'd never complained to me. While we were still talking, that is.

Our reunion had been engineered by tragedy. Her sister Skippie had overdosed the previous day, and Barb had reached out, just the way I had imagined she might someday. So, a weird sense of guilty culpability followed me to California. I knew it was ridiculous, but still. That's the way I'm built.

Barb is made of much sterner stuff. Which is why she's a regularly working television actress, or actor, as our acting coach used to prefer as a term for all. Yeah, we go way, way back.

We were, in fact, in it together for a long time. Our drama school programs had spit us out fresh as newborn babies into the hellish industry we aimed to conquer. We were luckier than most, as we had supportive, loving families at home, waiting for us to fail and come to our senses. We jostled elbows at auditions and while waiting tables with aspirants our age and younger who worked without a net, who were numbed to the ways they made desperate money to survive the dark edges of their dreams.

Still, we had had our share of, what shall I call them? Mishaps. This was all way before the #MeToo awakening. But these events were just a part of a larger canvas, the ugly of the good and the bad. When we got together, Barb and I would conjure a third, an entity we cultivated and celebrated called Us in our Twenties in L.A. Only we can raise this specter. I've missed it since she and I had a final falling out, fifteen years ago. Over a guy. Total cliché. But not the way you'd think. She didn't want Kenny; she was just jealous of the time he took away from my attention to her. I married him and left the state.

And I'm happier than I ever thought I could be. I feel oddly guilty about that, too, that I could find a conventional life so blissful.

I fight my way through the paparazzi who litter her perfect lawn and get waved ahead by a security guard. Soon. I'm close enough to breathe in her signature scent: L'Air du Temps. We embrace. Then, the smooth sharp curves of her new cheekbones, which still fit perfectly when cupped within my rough palms. Her face is flawless; it barely moves as her red eyes blur over with tears. *Midge,* she whispers. She pulls me inside and bolts the door behind us.

WOLFSBANE

First off, she wasn't exactly my grandma. Everyone in town called her that, a term of respect for those fortunate enough to survive to middle age. Though perhaps, given the realities of my youth, the word "fortunate" does little justice to the everyday brutality of our lives. "Hardy enough" is possibly more accurate. We killed what we had to, ate when we could, and survived the vagaries of our environment to the best of our ability. Most folks were ready to die when their time came.

And I wasn't exactly a sweet, knock-kneed little girl. Those berry-stained capes were a signal back then. I was a fully-fledged member of a club that was equal parts feared and reviled. And technically outlawed. That we were all anatomically female goes without saying, as anything a male did was axiomatically considered within his rights. No, transgression belonged to my sisters and me, as well as to those who identified with neither or both camps.

Our crimes were all of passion. We devoted ourselves to the health of those with child, aiming to upset the naturally cruel order of things by supplementing their nutrition enough to bring new life into our unforgiving midst. We had also learned how to assist the little ones as they arrived screaming between our outstretched palms. The sanctioned and the illicit, the weak and the strong, the typical and the unusual; all newborns were given our tender care in collaboration with their mothers, according to their wishes. When parental desires did not coincide with the well-being of the babes, we took them in as our own, and so, grew our ranks.

Our collective included only a single male-presenting child, as boys were highly valued treasures in our village. But Aaron, as I named him, was born feet-first, and judged responsible for his mother's death and later, his father's disappearance. I loved him from the moment he was released from the womb, silent and curled like a blanched seashell. I had snatched him away from the oaths of his vengeful older brother, who later followed his father's craven example.

Aaron was with me that day, and I remember his excitement at the prospect of displaying his hard-won musical mastery of the ram's horn Grandma had given him the year before. We had made three potato pies for her. She depended on the Red Hoods for food, especially in the wintertime. Her cottage was on the far side of town, near the forest, and I argued with Aaron about wearing warmer clothes for the trek; he had just turned ten and his burgeoning independence was beginning to test us both.

Halfway there, we lay our knapsacks of pie down on a frozen tree stump to rest and ate the apples we had packed. The wind had picked up, its icy fingers bleeding through the worn places in our cloaks and leggings. When I wordlessly pulled Aaron's fur-lined gloves out of my satchel and handed them to him, his blazing smile warmed me as no fire ever could.

Grandma's cottage came into view as the sun began to set. As we drew closer, I thought I heard a crash come from inside. I threw my arm across Aaron's chest to halt his progress and pointed downward. Boot prints in the snow. They originated from the adjacent forest and clustered around the well in Grandma's front yard. I judged five or six men had gathered there. More tracks led to her door. Woodsmen. The thought chilled me to the bone.

I was stirred to action by the sounds of obscenities yowled and pottery smashed. I half-dragged Aaron into the thicket. He was shaking with fear and the cold, but his eyes were steady as they met my own.

Wolfsbane, I whispered to my son. *For the pies. Be careful.* He was still for a moment, then held up his glove-protected hands to let me know he understood.

We had gathered the venomous purple flowers before. They had many therapeutic uses when prepared and deployed in tiny amounts by a trained practitioner. But the raw plants were poisonous even to the touch. Ingested, death was quick but agonizing.

It took no more than a few moments for us to locate a smattering of wolfsbane. We were able to lift the crusts off the pies and add the stems and petals to the potato fillings with a minimum of surface disturbance, though I doubted the food would be inspected before consumption. When we were finished, we sprinkled the plant's deadliest element, its seeds, over the top of each pie.

I bade my child stay put, and I crept from the woods to the cottage's hearth and deposited the pies there. I ran to the well; when I was close, I blew Aaron's prized ram's horn as loudly as I could before ducking behind its thick stonework.

The pillagers appeared in the doorway, and one of them shouted at the sight of the food. By the light of the moon, I saw the Woodsmen fall upon the pies like the animals they were.

The screams were dreadful as the men succumbed to our lethal recipe, and incapacitation did not take long. I beckoned Aaron from behind the tree line, and he joined me at the well. I handed the ram's horn to him; his nod told me he would use it to warn me if necessary. I stepped over the dying and went inside.

The Red Hoods' frantic search party found Aaron and me outside Grandma's cottage, huddled together in the lunar haze. We wept as one, our grief recognized and amplified by the local wolves, whose howls joined our own as they offered their soft bodies to us for warmth and comfort.

At dawn, we staggered to our feet. And we carried Grandma's ravaged body home, over the river and through the woods.

GRAVID/18 WEEKS

No gravity, she's as light as a feather we intoned, kneeling on our sleeping bags, placing our fingertips beneath her, all of us giddy on sisterhood and stolen beer. Rising, we chanted, lifting her high before we let go. We'd have an answer by morning, stay with her all night.

SHRINKWRAPPED

My sister's words came to mind, as they often did, when I needed them, and when they were the most unwelcome. Do you want to be right, or do you want to be married? I mulled over my options as I stuffed Kleenex into my handbag and left the ladies' lounge.

That evening, Sam and I were celebrating a friend's promotion at the hospital. Arlo was finally at the desk he'd always wanted, in a senior supervisory position; he and his wife Rennie were both psychologists and aimed to grow her private practice as he wound his down. Marnie and Ben were there too, an ambitious, fun couple only five years or so out of grad school. The six of us were maybe three drinks in, waiting for an overpriced meal at an over-hyped Boston restaurant. Sam had chosen it.

Marnie had just picked up the proofs of a wedding she'd been in, her maid-of-honor duties apparently extending to such matters. The photos were being passed around to get our opinions on their worthiness of inclusion in the all-important Album. I nearly said how little it would matter in a shockingly short amount of time, as such mementos' status subsided to baby journals, crayon drawings, and yearbooks. Instead, I ordered another drink and ignored Sam's sharp glance in my direction.

One photograph in particular caught our collective attention. It was a tight, casual shot of four couples, including Marnie and Ben. They were grouped closely together and beamed into the camera lens the purest kind of ferocity: lust and joy and vitality. You couldn't help but smile back.

Rennie broke the spell. She wondered which of the couples would get divorced first, and who would leave whom.

Marnie looked indignant, and I gathered these were friends she'd brought with her to her and Ben's marriage because Ben just laughed. He suggested we pool our bets; the winner and spouse would have dinner on everyone else at a later date. It was a weird proposal, and it didn't take multiple winners into consideration, or how on earth we'd ever substantiate who'd won, but we all seemed to be in what Sam would call a mood. Which I always thought was an odd thing for a psychiatrist to say; one might expect something more arcane from someone like him.

Arlo ordered another round of drinks and suggested some ground rules. We must base our choices on photographical clues alone and provide a reason why we deduced the relationship was doomed. No other intel was allowed; that'd be cheating, he said, looking at Marnie and Ben. He also graciously offered an exit ramp for me, the only non-shrink at the table. Rennie threw me a sympathetic look. I bared my teeth at him and said that I was all in, despite my feeble civilian status.

Sam guffawed. His take on my chosen profession was no secret. According to him, my career writing book reviews consisted of sitting in one place much too long for a normal person and making stuff up. I could have said the same of his line of work.

Our appetizers arrived with the beverages and the photo was circulated again, along with the pencils and paper we had begged from our beleaguered server. I rolled my eyes at the poor guy as he withdrew; in return, he saluted and did a vaudevillian kind of fake stumble.

Forty-five minutes and six entrees later, we made our bets.

Arlo went first. He pointed at the most dapper of the husbands and pointed out the guy's luxury branded wardrobe and jewelry. Arlo's theory was that he would eventually trade up, matrimonially. Our eyes went to the guy's wife, whose steely blues gazed confidently into the camera while gripping her husband's forearm; her knuckles were paled with the effort. I didn't think he was going anywhere.

Marnie speculated that a petite woman with dark hair might be untrustworthy and drew our attention to the fact that while everybody else looked directly at the camera, she seemed to be focused beyond it, grinning at someone in the wedding crowd facing them all. Rennie cried foul, saying Marnie was operating with privileged information, as only she and Ben would know the physical setup.

And so we continued, through coffee.

I felt fairly confident when it was my turn. I chose one of the husbands in a dark suit with curly hair and stylishly old-fashioned glasses; I told our party that I thought he was already cheating on the wife at his side. If you look closely, I said, the woman's lipstick was terribly smeared above her mouth. Her husband either didn't care enough to tell her or hadn't bothered to notice it before they all posed for the professional photographer.

Nobody said anything for a minute. I couldn't help but feel a bit smug as I excused myself to go to the powder room. Where I discovered the swatch of toothpaste on my chin. It had hardened into a greenish blur during the four hours since I'd brushed my teeth at home with Sam. I chipped it off and headed back to the dining room.

The table was laughing at a story of Arlo's as I sat back down and joined the conversation. The contest was never mentioned again, not that evening, and not ever at any of our subsequent gatherings. Sam gets home earlier from work these days, and I try to get out from behind my computer more often. And Rennie and I broke off our affair. Life is less complicated now, in a good way, I think.

SUGAR, SUGAR

Liza is a five-year-old ball of fury at my elbow as we wait in line at the grocery store. She tries again.

"Moomah, just this! Just this, please!"

And I tell her again that we already have plenty of sweets at home.

"But this is special," she moans, waving a fistful of bright yellow bars. "Abby gave me some of hers at school and they're so good! They're called Butterfingers and I found them here!"

"Next time," I tell her.

When it's our turn at the cashier's, she squeezes past me and waits with the paper bags at the end of the conveyor belt. She won't look at me.

I'm sorting the last of our groceries when out of the corner of my eye I detect quick motion. I glance surreptitiously at Liza. She is focused on her own outstretched palms. She kisses each one a few times, then does a little dance with her hands; it looks like she's releasing doves. Then she kisses her fingertips and mumbles a few words under her breath. With a start I realize that my younger daughter has just cast a spell. On me.

I look away. The moment belongs to her alone.

We load up the car and head back to the house. When I pull into a random driveway halfway home and turn around, Liza notices and asks me why.

"I'm not sure," I say. "I just suddenly have, like, a super strong urge to go back to the store and get those Butterfinger bars."

I watch her in the rearview mirror as she absorbs this information. Her eyes are huge round Os. She presses her lips tightly together and sucks them inside her mouth, trying her hardest not to broadcast her glee.

"Okay," she says, mildly.

Years later, I ask her about it. She has no memory of that trip. But for me, it remains the best candy I've ever eaten, our car party of two crunching chocolate all the way home, Liza with a bar for her big sister clutched in a grubby fist, each ecstatic in our own way.

STILL

"Be still," he yells at me from behind the wheel as he savagely cuts the engine. In the back seat, I tremble while the state trooper peers through the window and asks terrible, irrelevant questions of my new father-in-law. Where were you and with whom and what time? My husband's mother is silent, but her eyes are kind as she turns to me, her finger across her lips like a crucifix. I mean to tell their son about it when I get home, but I don't. I stay still. And I wonder just how far poisoned fruit can possibly fall.

COLD

I'm in bed half asleep when I hear something. My industrial-strength curtains are pulled closed against the San Francisco summer cold, so I can't see a thing. Heavy, uneven steps are getting closer, and I reach next to the nightstand for the baseball bat I acquired when we moved last year from the Mission to the Tenderloin.

Dim light escapes from the hallway as the door swings open, and Patrick is standing there. I put the bat away. He looks at me from behind a half-mask, the sparkly kind you buy at a Mardi Gras parade, and I don't know if this is a prank, or he's broken up with Amy, or we're back where we were a year ago.

"Gimme your guitar," he says.

Okay. We're back.

"You know I can't do that," I say. "It's me. It's how I pay the rent. And right now she's my girlfriend."

"That's disgusting," says Patrick. "I'm still taking her."

I get up and switch on a lamp to get a better look at him and damn if he isn't a horror show. He's shaking and sweating so much I can see tiny gray droplets shiver off his face and arms and onto the rug we thrifted together from the Goodwill down the corner. He wipes his nose and stares at me, his eyes watery and wide, but fierce.

"Since when?" I ask. I don't need to elaborate.

Patrick slams his way in, nearly falling. When he lifts his head up again, he radiates the charisma of a kindergarten teacher or a death cult prophet.

"Don't make me rip everything apart," he tells me.

There's nothing I can say that he can tolerate right now. I grab my phone from under my pillow.

"If you call Amy, I'll kill you," he says.

We've known each other since high school, and while I don't really think he's capable of hurting me, I don't know exactly what he's on besides his old friend, H, and so I put the phone down on the rug between us and raise my hands, palms out.

"Take the phone," I tell him.

"That's a piece of shit," he says.

This is true. It's a burner, one of a series I've bought since Patrick "borrowed and lost" a couple of iPhones.

I drop to the floor and sit crisscross applesauce, as my sisters used to say. Patrick looks startled by this feat of flexibility and leans against the crumbling wallpaper, whose obscenely blooming calla lilies had made us grin like schoolboys when we first toured the apartment.

"How can I help?" I ask.

When I come to, I'm in a narrow hospital bed with tubes in my arm that lead to a bag of clear liquid. Amy is talking. Her small frame is swallowed up by the upholstered armchair someone must have smuggled in for her. *UCSF* is stamped onto its faux leather in block letters, so at least I know where I am.

"Take it easy," she says, like I have any plans to do anything but lie here in the worst pain I've ever been in, worse than breaking my ankle in three places playing soccer, worse than knocking out a few teeth snowboarding on a cafeteria tray in college. My eyes are so swollen I'm looking at her through horizontal peepholes.

"I'll tell them you're awake," says Amy. "Maybe if you talk to them, they'll give you some painkillers; they said they need to talk to your regular doctor beforehand or get the results of your bloodwork, whichever comes first. Because of Patrick's...condition."

"Where is he?" I manage.

"He's here, too. ICU," she says.

"What happened?"

Amy leans in and speaks softly as she tells me how a neighbor called 911 because of the noise, and when the cops got to the apartment, I was unconscious and Patrick was ransacking the place. He had tried to run but stumbled on the stairs and fell, hitting his head. His prognosis is an open question. She had called both our families.

I try to take it all in while Amy looks for a nurse. She's gone a few minutes and then comes back with an apple juice carton, opened and strawed.

"He find Lucille?"

My guitar. Yeah, just like B.B. King. The best of the best.

"She wasn't with Patrick," says Amy, "so I guess not."

I follow her gaze; she's looking at my hands which, like lots of the rest of me, are screaming, throbbing like hellfire itself inside stiff pale bandages.

"He went for them with your bat," she says.

I nod.

"So, he knows, I guess?"

Amy gets into the bed and, carefully, so carefully, puts her arms around me.

"I guess he does," she whispers.

DEATH AND OTHER SURVIVAL STRATEGIES

The two might have been sisters, both sharp-boned and pale with worry inside their shapeless featherweight dresses. Lettered tiles dozed on the table between them, grazed by the same fetid breeze that flicked at the spindly plants on their windowsill.

"Another epic battle of wits ends predictably. Brava!" said Laurel.

"I had some lucky breaks."

"If you say so," said Laurel. She paused for a moment. "We do need to get to our paperwork, though. We can't keep putting it off."

Iris closed her eyes and nodded. She became very still. Laurel could feel her mother telescoping backwards through memory and time.

"Mom, I'm sorry. But listen, we need to make some decisions. It won't get any easier. And if we miss the deadline, it'll lessen your chances of, of…"

"Beating out the competition?"

"I know. It's ugly," said Laurel. "At least we won't know which Academies your friends get into. I'd like to never know when it's my time."

Iris took a long breath, so shallow that the movement barely registered beneath her clothing. Laurel moved closer and placed a gentle hand over her mother's.

"You okay? Where are you on the pain scale?"

"Not a smiley face, but not too bad. Mostly, I'm tired."

"I know it. I'm so sorry. But if we don't even apply..." Laurel's voice sounded shrill to her own ears, and she willed herself to stay calm.

"No, I understand," said Iris.

A staccato flurry of small explosions erupted, followed by the shrieks and joyful howls of the crowd celebrating on the scraggy beach across the street. It had become dark enough for the fireworks to begin. Iris glanced wearily in the direction of the noise before Laurel tried again.

"So. We're done with the recommendations, right? Those testimonial forms? Unless you have any more coming in ..."

Iris looked away before speaking.

"Nathan said he'd do one, but I haven't been able to reach him since. I do have some new papers for you to sign. Typical bureaucratic bullshit waivers."

"Mom!" The mock outrage was a habit of theirs.

The two grinned at each other, and Iris managed a laugh.

"I'll take a look at those later," said Laurel. "How about now I read aloud the descriptions of the ones you might want to consider? Each Academy has a different angle."

"Agenda."

The righteous contempt in her mother's voice set something loose in her chest. Laurel willed herself not to cry.

"Yes, agenda."

"Sorry. Go on."

Laurel chose a random brochure from the print collection she had stacked on top of the Scrabble box.

"Marshpoint needs an interesting or obscure disease they can study. Doctors get total access. But the quality of life there is very high."

"Makes sense. Pampering the lab rats. But why is this one on our list? Cancer's as common as mud."

"Well," said Laurel carefully, "I was thinking that maybe we could get Dr. Atwood to sign off on a weird variation. I think he'd do it for us. He's already fifty himself."

"Honey, we can't ask him. You know what would happen to him if he was caught. Also."

"Also?"

"I learned something a few weeks ago. I didn't want to trouble you with it."

"Tell me."

"Turns out Aunt Hannah didn't have Koenig's Virus. An honest misdiagnosis. But she was judged...useless. Her doctor's okay. But Hannah was, was..."

Laurel rose to hug her mother, whose thin arms wrapped around her neck with a surprisingly strenuous grip. She hoped it was a sign of Iris's characteristic tenacity and that it might carry her through the next few critical hours.

"Lord, that's awful. I never got to know her well. I wish she'd lived closer," Laurel murmured.

"Hannah was charged with falsifying her application."

"Okay," said Laurel, settling back into her chair, "we don't go that route."

"No," said Iris.

"Here's the form for that Travel Academy. Four Winds. Jen's dad got into that program. He was able to get a letter out to her. He ended up in one of the new Greek states monitoring Kitsin levels."

"Monitoring?"

"Well, not exactly. Experiencing and reporting. But he wrote that the place is a paradise."

"Except for the poison gas."

"Yeah. Except for that."

The two women looked at each other and started to giggle, helplessly, then hysterically. The tears they had both been trying their best to conserve followed. When they were able to collect themselves, they used the hems of their light summer shifts to wipe their eyes.

"Evensong," said Laurel, pulling out a new folder. "They want special skills that can be taught. Like being a master chef, or clothes maker, or welding expert."

"I've never thought of myself as being especially talented. Except when it came to raising you, of course."

"The law was one and done. You had to make it count."

"And now for most people even one is too many! Ha!" snorted Iris. "Can you imagine if I applied to Evensong with procreation as my special skill?"

"They'd send you to the Academy for Impaired Elders and you'd be smoke the next day!"

Laurel covered her mouth, horrified. Her mind was a shiny blank space; she couldn't think of a word to say. Iris leaned over and caressed her daughter's face; her fingertips lingered there, their touch the feather of a kiss and the weight of a prayer.

She spoke softly. "Someone mentioned there was a new one, an Academy for Lost Languages. Is it on our list? I still speak a fair amount of Portuguese, though I can't say I was ever very good at it."

"Mom," said Laurel, jumping to her feet. "Let's just run. Please? Please."

"I'm not sure the running would do us any good," said Iris. "How about if we swim?"

"Swim?"

"It's the Fourth of July," said Iris. "Let's go to the beach."

Laurel nodded. She began to move about the small cottage, collecting things for their straw carryall. She was rummaging in her mother's closet for a swimsuit when she felt Iris behind her.

"No need," she said.

• • •

They ran like children into the waves, holding hands and screaming with the impact of the cold seawater. Laurel waited to watch the sun bleed its neon orange against the sky, hours later, over the littered expanse of sandy grit; no one bothered to clean up anymore, to pretend it mattered. She wondered what ever would again.

A Mourning in Wisconsin

Beccah let her shoulders relax and her head droop between them as she waited for her bucket to fill, a rare luxury possible only because Russ, her seven-year-old nephew, was visiting; he was young enough to think working the pump was fun and old enough to be able to manage it. She was only three times his age, but days like today, she felt ancient, curdled with a conviction that unless she did something unthinkable, she was staked for life. She looked over her shoulder at the house, mostly sod but real timber in some spots; by the time her husband rebuilt the whole place, Beccah reckoned she would have had three more besides the one in her belly. She raised her eyes to the horizon and calculated; she could be in town by nightfall if she started walking now. Russ put his small hand on her wrist before passing her the water she needed to prepare breakfast for the farmhands. She sang to him as they crossed the dusty yard, a tuneless rhyme about needful things, like rain, like fire, like yesterdays.

Light Blue

I'd never chosen a name for anything in my life before picking one out for my daughter. Not a single pet or toy or plant had been mine to decide. So, I always felt a thrill of satisfaction whenever I heard it because against all odds, it had turned out to be perfect for her. Aurora. Which is just to say that an hour after she called to tell me she had legally changed it to Citizen Twelve (there was some other nonsense too, about a desert religious cult she had joined and would I consider converting my worldly goods into cash and joining her) was not a great time to find policemen knocking at my door, one of them flashing his badge through the side window with the crack in it I'd asked Bob to repair a million times but he never did, just added it to a special household spreadsheet so he could keep track of all the things he wasn't taking care of. Which doesn't bother me, I mean, for better or worse, right? But, like, these cops outside look ready for anything. Maybe if I get Bob a cool uniform. And a utility belt. I hear the deck slider slam open and turn in time to see Bob's plaid-shirted back racing across the backyard. I can see this from the front door because of our home's great feng shui, which I hadn't noticed but which had been enthusiastically pointed out by our realtor when we'd bought the place. She had flirted with Bob outrageously, by the way. And even for California, she'd been hardly dressed as a professional, what with the tight strapless top and tiny pencil skirt. I did like her perfume though. Light Blue. I got some for myself and I swear, it smells so good I think Bob borrows it sometimes. The cops are being all pushy now, even after I tell them that Bob's just gone out, and when I finally open the door, one shoves some paper at me while the others scatter around the place. One comes back and asks what that smell is, and I tell him Light Blue perfume, but he says he's not talking about perfume; he's talking about a nasty odor, especially on the second floor. I tell the cop about Bob's spreadsheet and how he had told me about the decomposing squirrel in our attic and that he had promised to move the issue into top position. I get asked about Bob's boss then, who we had over for supper recently, and when did I last see him. I explain that the guys had stayed up late, and I had gone to bed. And no, I didn't see him leave. But Bob was really cheerful the next day, so I guess they had fun. The phone rings then and the cops tell me to answer it and it's my daughter and she's asking me to come to the desert again, and I'm thinking maybe the dry heat would be good for my arthritis and that it might be interesting to be Citizen Thirteen for at least a while as my neighbors are currently on our front lawn talking to reporters and they look grumpy and I'm worried they'll tell the cops about our illegal garbage disposal. Which is a very big deal in this town.

Coda

After tomorrow, none of it would matter; I had plans that didn't include me.

Acknowledgements

Thank you, my awesome beta readers, lovely friends, and wonderful family; my gratitude for your encouragement and support is beyond words. Team Vine Leaves Press, you are the best! A special shout out to Jessica Bell and Amie McCracken, and my VLP editors Melanie Faith and Melissa Slayton, whose input has been invaluable. And enormous thanks to Paula Breger, Connie Hambley, Elizabeth Rose, Bonnie Leflore, and Linda Sanchez, without whom I could not have finished this book.

Many of the stories in this collection were first published by the wonderful editors of the following literary journals and magazines:

"Full Moon," *ActiveMuse Literary Journal*
"Last Shift at Dollar Haven," "A Visitation," and "NYC 1987," *Blink-Ink*
"The Blouse," *Blue Animal Literature*
"Raising Girls Who Make Waves," *The Boston Globe*
"Seventeenth and Clay," *Bridge Eight Press*
"Shrinkwrapped," *Brilliant Flash Fiction*
"Still," *The Centifictionist*
"All Hallows' Eve," and "Triquetra," *Club Plum Literary Journal*
"Wolfsbane," *Daikaijuzine*
"I Know What You're Going to Say," *Dime Show Review*

"Undone," and "Waiting on the World to Change," *The Dribble Drabble Review*

"Cherry Bones," and "Two Sisters in the Louvre," *The Ekphrastic Review*

"Grit," *Eunoia Review*

"The Calling," *Fiction Kitchen Berlin*

"August and All That," "By Dawn's Early Light," "On the 495 North," "Reception," "Released," and "Something Blue," *50-Word Stories*

"In a New York Market," and "Packing It In," *Flash Fiction Magazine*

"A Dish Best Served Cold," *Friday Flash Fiction*

"True List of Things I Believed as a Child, In No Particular Order," *HASH Journal*

"Constrained by Love," *K'in*

"Two Cups of Coffee," *Litro*

"Bargains," *Lowestoft Chronicle*

"Grounded," *Microfiction Monday Magazine*

"Sugar, Sugar," *Motherwell Magazine*;

"Fairytale Wedding," *Orca: A Literary Journal*

"Rhetoric 101," *Paragraph Planet*

"Distant, Socially," *Reflex Press*

"Agave Cotton," "Communion," "Folie a Deux," "Lunch Ticket," and "My Zaide's Golem," *Six Sentences*

"Lovely in the Dying Light," and "Suburban," *Tales from the Moonlit Path*

"Road Show," *Wanderlust Journal*

Best of the Net nominee, "Border Town," *The Wild Word*

ALSO BY CAROLYN R. RUSSELL

Q & A
In the Fullness of Time
The Films of Joel and Ethan Coen